The Collected Supernatural and Weird Fiction of E. G. Swain

—The Stoneground Ghost Tales—

&

Ralph Adams Cram

—Black Spirits and White—

The Collected
Supernatural and Weird
Fiction of
E. G. Swain
—The Stoneground Ghost Tales—

&

Ralph Adams Cram
—Black Spirits and White—

Fifteen Short Tales
to Chill the Blood

E. G. Swain

&

Ralph Adams Cram

LEONAUR

The Collected
Supernatural and Weird
Fiction of
E. G. Swain
—The Stoneground Ghost Tales—
&
Ralph Adams Cram
—Black Spirits and White—

Fifteen Short Tales
to Chill the Blood
by E. G. Swain
&
Ralph Adams Cram

First published under the title
The Stoneground Ghost Tales
and
Black Spirits and White

Leonaur is an imprint of Oakpast Ltd

Copyright in this form © 2011 Oakpast Ltd

ISBN: 978-0-85706-084-6 (hardcover)
ISBN: 978-0-85706-083-9 (softcover)

http://www.leonaur.com

Contents

The Stoneground Ghost Tales   7

Black Spirits and White   125

The Stoneground Ghost Tales

E. G. Swain

Contents

The Man With the Roller   11

Bone to His Bone   21

The Richpins   31

The Eastern Window   48

Lubrietta   60

The Rockery   72

The Indian Lampshade   84

The Place of Safery   99

The Kirk Spook   116

The Man With the Roller

On the edge of that vast tract of East Anglia, which retains its ancient name of the Fens, there may be found, by those who know where to seek it, a certain village called Stoneground. It was once a picturesque village. Today it is not to be called either a village, or picturesque. Man dwells not in one "house of clay," but in two, and the material of the second is drawn from the earth upon which this and the neighbouring villages stood. The unlovely signs of the industry have changed the place alike in aspect and in population. Many who have seen the fossil skeletons of great saurians brought out of the clay in which they have lain from prehistoric times, have thought that the inhabitants of the place have not since changed for the better. The chief habitations, however, have their foundations not upon clay, but upon a bed of gravel which anciently gave to the place its name, and upon the highest part of this gravel stands, and has stood for many centuries, the Parish church, dominating the landscape for miles around.

Stoneground, however, is no longer the inaccessible village, which in the middle ages stood out above a waste of waters. Occasional floods serve to indicate what was once its ordinary outlook, but in more recent times the construction of roads and railways, and the drainage of the Fens, have given it freedom of communication with the world from which it was formerly isolated.

The vicarage of Stoneground stands hard by the church, and is renowned for its spacious garden, part of which, and that (as might be expected) the part nearest the house, is of ancient date. To the original plot successive vicars have added adjacent lands, so that the garden has gradually acquired the state in which it now appears.

The vicars have been many in number. Since Henry de Greville was instituted in the year 1140 there have been thirty, all of whom have lived, and most of whom have died, in successive vicarage houses upon the present site.

The present incumbent, Mr. Batchel, is a solitary man of somewhat studious habits, but is not too much enamoured of his solitude to receive visits, from time to time, from schoolboys and such. In the summer of the year 1906 he entertained two, who are the occasion of this narrative, though still unconscious of their part in it, for one of the two, celebrating his 15th birthday during his visit to Stoneground, was presented by Mr. Batchel with a new camera, with which he proceeded to photograph, with considerable skill, the surroundings of the house.

One of these photographs Mr. Batchel thought particularly pleasing. It was a view of the house with the lawn in the foreground. A few small copies, such as the boy's camera was capable of producing, were sent to him by his young friend, some weeks after the visit, and again Mr. Batchel was so much pleased with the picture, that he begged for the negative, with the intention of having the view enlarged.

The boy met the request with what seemed a needlessly modest plea. There were two negatives, he replied, but each of them had, in the same part of the picture, a small blur for which there was no accounting otherwise than by carelessness. His desire, therefore, was to discard these films, and to produce something more worthy of enlargement, upon a subsequent visit.

Mr. Batchel, however, persisted in his request, and upon receipt of the negative, examined it with a lens. He was just able to detect the blur alluded to; an examination under a powerful glass, in fact revealed something more than he had at first detected. The blur was like the nucleus of a comet as one sees it represented in pictures, and seemed to be connected with a faint streak which extended across the negative. It was, however, so inconsiderable a defect that Mr. Batchel resolved to disregard it. He had a neighbour whose favourite pastime was photography, one who was notably skilled in everything that pertained to the art, and to him he sent the negative, with the request for an enlargement, reminding him of a long-standing promise to do any such service, when as had now happened, his friend might see fit to ask it.

This neighbour who had acquired such skill in photography was one Mr. Groves, a young clergyman, residing in the precincts of the minster near at hand, which was visible from Mr. Batchel's garden. He lodged with a Mrs. Rumney, a superannuated servant of the palace, and a strong-minded vigorous woman still, exactly such a one as Mr. Groves needed to have about him. For he was a constant trial to Mrs. Rumney, and but for the wholesome fear she begot in him, would have converted his rooms into a mere den. Her carpets and tablecloths were continually bespattered with chemicals; her chimney-piece ornaments had been unceremoniously stowed away and replaced by labelled bottles; even the bed of Mr, Groves was, by day, strewn with drying films and mounts, and her old and favourite cat had a bald patch on his flank, the result of a mishap with the pyrogallic acid.

Mrs. Rumney's lodger, however, was a great favourite with her, as such helpless men are apt to be with motherly women, and she took no small pride in his work. A life-size portrait of herself, originally a peace-offering, hung in her parlour, and had long excited the envy of every friend who took tea with her.

"Mr. Groves," she was wont to say, "is a nice gentleman, AND a gentleman; and chemical though he may be, I'd rather wait on him for nothing than what I would on anyone else for twice the money."

Every new piece of photographic work was of interest to Mrs. Rumney, and she expected to be allowed both to admire and to criticise. The view of Stoneground Vicarage, therefore, was shewn to her upon its arrival. "Well may it want enlarging," she remarked, "and it no bigger than a postage stamp; it looks more like a doll's house than a vicarage," and with this she went about her work, whilst Mr. Groves retired to his dark room with the film, to see what he could make of the task assigned to him.

Two days later, after repeated visits to his dark room, he had made something considerable; and when Mrs. Rumney brought him his chop for luncheon, she was lost in admiration. A large but unfinished print stood upon his easel, and such a picture of Stoneground Vicarage was in the making as was calculated to delight both the young photographer and the vicar.

Mr. Groves spent only his mornings, as a rule, in photography. His afternoons he gave to pastoral work, and the work upon this enlargement was over for the day. It required, little more than "touching up," but it was this "touching up" which made the difference between the enlargements of Mr. Groves and those of other men. The print, therefore, was to be left upon the easel until the morrow, when it was to be finished. Mrs. Rumney and he, together, gave it an admiring inspection as she was carrying away the tray, and what they agreed in admiring most particularly was the smooth and open stretch of lawn, which made so excellent a foreground for the picture "It looks," said Mrs. Rumney, who had once been young, "as if it was waiting for someone to come and dance on it."

Mr. Groves left his lodgings—we must now be particular about the hours—at half-past two, with the intention of returning, as usual, at five. "As reg'lar as a clock," Mrs. Rumney was wont to say, "and a sight more reg'lar than some clocks I knows of."

Upon this day he was, nevertheless, somewhat late, some visit had detained him unexpectedly, and it was a quarter-past five when he inserted his latch-key in Mrs. Rumney's door.

Hardly had he entered, when his landlady, obviously awaiting him, appeared in the passage: her face, usually florid, was of the colour of parchment, and, breathing hurriedly and shortly, she pointed at the door of Mr. Groves' room.

In some alarm at her condition, Mr. Groves hastily questioned her; all she could say was: "The photograph! the photograph!" Mr. Groves could only suppose that his enlargement had met with some mishap for which Mrs. Rumney was responsible. Perhaps she had allowed it to flutter into the fire. He turned towards his room in order to discover the worst, but at this Mrs. Rumney laid a trembling hand upon his arm, and held him back. "Don't go in," she said, "have your tea in the parlour."

"Nonsense," said Mr. Groves, "if that is gone we can easily do another."

"Gone," said his landlady, "I wish to Heaven it was."

The ensuing conversation shall not detain us. It will suffice to say that after a considerable time Mr. Groves succeeded in quieting his landlady, so much so that she consented, still trembling violently, to enter the room with him. To speak truth, she was as much concerned for him as for herself, and she was not by nature a timid woman.

The room, so far from disclosing to Mr. Groves any cause for excitement, appeared wholly unchanged. In its usual place stood every article of his stained and ill-used furniture, on the easel stood the photograph, precisely where he had left it; and except that his tea was not upon the table, everything was in its usual state and place.

But Mrs. Rumney again became excited and tremulous, "It's there," she cried. "Look at the lawn."

Mr. Groves stepped quickly forward and looked at the photograph. Then he turned as pale as Mrs. Rumney herself.

There was a man, a man with an indescribably horrible suffering face, rolling the lawn with a large roller.

Mr. Groves retreated in amazement to where Mrs. Rumney had remained standing. "Has anyone been in here?" he asked.

"Not a soul," was the reply, "I came in to make up the fire, and turned to have another look at the picture, when I saw that dead-alive face at the edge. It gave me the creeps," she said, "particularly from not having noticed it before. If that's anyone in Stoneground, I said to myself, I wonder the vicar has him in the garden with that awful face. It took that hold of me I thought

I must come and look at it again, and at five o'clock I brought your tea in. And then I saw him moved along right in front, with a roller dragging behind him, like you see.

Mr. Groves was greatly puzzled. Mrs. Rumney's story, of course, was incredible, but this strange evil-faced man had appeared in the photograph somehow. That he had not been there when the print was made was quite certain.

The problem soon ceased to alarm Mr. Groves; in his mind it was investing itself with a scientific interest. He began to think of suspended chemical action, and other possible avenues of investigation. At Mrs. Rumney's urgent entreaty, however, he turned the photograph upon the easel, and with only its white back presented to the room, he sat down and ordered tea to be brought in.

He did not look again at the picture. The face of the man had about it something unnaturally painful: he could remember, and still see, as it were, the drawn features, and the look of the man had unaccountably distressed him.

He finished his slight meal, and having lit a pipe, began to brood over the scientific possibilities of the problem. Had any other photograph upon the original film become involved in the one he had enlarged? Had the image of any other face, distorted by the enlarging lens, become a part of this picture? For the space of two hours he debated this possibility, and that, only to reject them all. His optical knowledge told him that no conceivable accident could have brought into his picture a man with a roller. No negative of his had ever contained such a man; if it had, no natural causes would suffice to leave him, as it were, hovering about the apparatus.

His repugnance to the actual thing had by this time lost its freshness, and he determined to end his scientific musings with another inspection of the object. So he approached the easel and turned the photograph round again. His horror returned, and with good cause. The man with the roller had now advanced to the middle of the lawn. The face was stricken still with the same indescribable look of suffering. The man seemed to be appealing to the spectator for some kind of help. Almost, he spoke.

Mr. Groves was naturally reduced to a condition of extreme nervous excitement. Although not by nature what is called a nervous man, he trembled from head to foot. With a sudden effort, he turned away his head, took hold of the picture with his outstretched hand, and opening a drawer in his sideboard thrust the thing underneath a folded tablecloth which was lying there. Then he closed the drawer and took up an entertaining book to distract his thoughts from the whole matter.

In this he succeeded very ill. Yet somehow the rest of the evening passed, and as it wore away, he lost something of his alarm. At ten o'clock, Mrs. Rumney, knocking and receiving answer twice, lest by any chance she should find herself alone in the room, brought in the cocoa usually taken by her lodger at that hour. A hasty glance at the easel showed her that it stood empty, and her face betrayed her relief. She made no comment, and Mr. Groves invited none.

The latter, however, could not make up his mind to go to bed. The face he had seen was taking firm hold upon his imagination, and seemed to fascinate him and repel him at the same time. Before long, he found himself wholly unable to resist the impulse to look at it once more. He took it again, with some indecision, from the drawer and laid it under the lamp.

The man with the roller had now passed completely over the lawn, and was near the left of the picture.

The shock to Mr. Groves was again considerable. He stood facing the fire, trembling with excitement which refused to be suppressed. In this state his eye lighted upon the calendar hanging before him, and it furnished him with some distraction. The next day was his mother's birthday. Never did he omit to write a letter which should lie upon her breakfast-table, and the preoccupation of this evening had made him wholly forgetful of the matter. There was a collection of letters, however, from the pillar-box near at hand, at a quarter before midnight, so he turned to his desk, wrote a letter which would at least serve to convey his affectionate greetings, and having written it, went out into the night and posted it.

The clocks were striking midnight as he returned to his room. We may be sure that he did not resist the desire to glance at the photograph he had left on his table. But the results of that glance, he, at any rate, had not anticipated. The man with the roller had disappeared.

The lawn lay as smooth and clear as at first, "looking," as Mrs. Rumney had said, "as if it was waiting for someone to come and dance on it."

The photograph, after this, remained a photograph and nothing more. Mr. Groves would have liked to persuade himself that it had never undergone these changes which he had witnessed, and which we have endeavoured to describe, but his sense of their reality was too insistent. He kept the print lying for a week upon his easel. Mrs. Rumney, although she had ceased to dread it, was obviously relieved at its disappearance, when it was carried to Stoneground to be delivered to Mr. Batchel. Mr. Groves said nothing of the man with the roller, but gave the enlargement, without comment, into his friend's hands. The work of enlargement had been skilfully done, and was deservedly praised.

Mr. Groves, making some modest disclaimer, observed that the view, with its spacious foreground of lawn, was such as could not have failed to enlarge well. And this lawn, he added, as they sat looking out of the vicar's study, looks as well from within your house as from without. It must give you a sense of responsibility, he added, reflectively, to be sitting where your predecessors have sat for so many centuries and to be continuing their peaceful work. The mere presence before your window, of the turf upon which good men have walked, is an inspiration.

The vicar made no reply to these somewhat sententious remarks. For a moment he seemed as if he would speak some words of conventional assent. Then he abruptly left the room, to return in a few minutes with a parchment book.

"Your remark, Groves," he said as he seated himself again, "recalled to me a curious bit of history: I went up to the old library to get the book. This is the journal of William Longue who was vicar here up to the year 1602. What you said about the lawn will give you an interest in a certain portion of the journal. I will read it."

Aug. 1, 1600.—I am now returned in haste from a journey to Brightelmstone whither I had gone with full intention to remain about the space of two months. Master Josiah Wilburton, of my dear College of Emmanuel, having consented to assume the charge of my parish of Stoneground in the meantime. But I had intelligence, after twelve days' absence, by a messenger from the churchwardens, that Master Wilburton had disappeared last Monday sennight, and had been no more seen. So here I am again in my study to the entire frustration of my plans, and can do nothing in my perplexity but sit and look out from my window, before which Andrew Birch rolleth the grass with much persistence. Andrew passeth so many times over the same place with his roller that I have just now stepped without to demand why he so wasteth his labour, and upon this he hath pointed out a place which is not levelled, and hath continued his rolling.

Aug. 2.—There is a change in Andrew Birch since my absence, who hath indeed the aspect of one in great depression, which is noteworthy of so cheerful a man. He haply shares our common trouble in respect of Master Wilburton, of whom we remain without tidings. Having made part of a sermon upon the seventh chapter of the former Epistle of St. Paul to the Corinthians and the 27th verse, I found Andrew again at his task, and bade him desist and saddle my horse, being minded to ride forth and take counsel with my good friend John Palmer at the Deanery, who bore Master Wilburton great affection.

Aug. 2 continued.—Dire news awaiteth me upon my return. The sheriff's men have disinterred the body of poor Master W. from beneath the grass Andrew was rolling, and have arrested him on the charge of being his cause of death.

Aug. 10.—Alas! Andrew Birch hath been hanged, the Justice having mercifully ordered that he should hang by the neck until he should be dead, and not sooner molested. May the Lord have mercy on his soul. He made full confession before me, that he had slain Master Wilburton in heat upon his threatening to make me privy to certain peculation of which I should not have suspected so old a servant. The poor man bemoaned his evil temper in great contrition, and beat his breast, saying that he knew himself doomed for ever to roll the grass in the place where he had tried to conceal his wicked fact.

"Thank you," said Mr. Groves. "Has that little negative got the date upon it?"

"Yes, replied Mr. Batchel, as he examined it with his glass. The boy has marked it August 10. The vicar seemed not to re-mark the coincidence with the date of Birch's execution. Need-less to say that it did not escape Mr. Groves. But he kept silence about the man with the roller, who has been no more seen to this day.

Doubtless there is more in our photography than we yet know of. The camera sees more than the eye, and chemicals in a freshly prepared and active state, have a power which they afterwards lose. Our units of time, adopted for the convenience of persons dealing with the ordinary movements of material objects, are of course conventional. Those who turn the instruments of science upon nature will always be in danger of seeing more than they looked for. There is such a disaster as that of knowing too much, and at some time or another it may overtake each of us. May we then be as wise as Mr. Groves in our reticence, if our turn should come.

Bone to His Bone

William Whitehead, Fellow of Emmanuel College, in the University of Cambridge, became Vicar of Stoneground in the year 1731. The annals of his incumbency were doubtless short and simple: they have not survived. In his day were no newspapers to collect gossip, no parish magazines to record the simple events of parochial life. One event, however, of greater moment then than now, is recorded in two places. Vicar Whitehead failed in health after 23 years of work, and journeyed to Bath in what his monument calls "the vain hope of being restored." The duration of his visit is unknown; it is reasonable to suppose that he made his journey in the summer, it is certain that by the month of November his physician told him to lay aside all hope of recovery.

Then it was that the thoughts of the patient turned to the comfortable straggling vicarage he had left at Stoneground, in which he had hoped to end his days. He prayed that his successor might be as happy there as he had been himself. Setting his affairs in order, as became one who had but a short time to live, he executed a will, bequeathing to the Vicars of Stoneground, forever, the close of ground he had recently purchased because it lay next the vicarage garden. And by a codicil, he added to the bequest his library of books. Within a few days, William Whitehead was gathered to his fathers.

A mural tablet in the north aisle of the church, records, in Latin, his services and his bequests, his two marriages, and his fruitless journey to Bath. The house he loved, but never again saw, was taken down forty years later, and rebuilt by Vicar James Devie. The garden, with Vicar Whitehead's "close of ground" and other adjacent lands, was opened out and planted, somewhat before 1860, by Vicar Robert Towerson. The aspect of everything has changed. But in a convenient chamber on the first floor of the present vicarage the library of Vicar Whitehead stands very much as he used it and loved it, and as he bequeathed it to his successors "forever."

The books there are arranged as he arranged and ticketed them. Little slips of paper, sometimes bearing interesting fragments of writing, still mark his places. His marginal comments still give life to pages from which all other interest has faded, and he would have but a dull imagination who could sit in the chamber amidst these books without ever being carried back 180 years into the past, to the time when the newest of them left the printer's hands.

Of those into whose possession the books have come, some have doubtless loved them more, and some less; some, perhaps, have left them severely alone. But neither those who loved them, nor those who loved them not, have lost them, and they passed, some century and a half after William Whitehead's death, into the hands of Mr. Batchel, who loved them as a father loves his children. He lived alone, and had few domestic cares to distract his mind. He was able, therefore, to enjoy to the full what Vicar Whitehead had enjoyed so long before him. During many a long summer evening would he sit poring over long-forgotten books; and since the chamber, otherwise called the library, faced the south, he could also spend sunny winter mornings there without discomfort. Writing at a small table, or reading as he stood at a tall desk, he would browse amongst the books like an ox in a pleasant pasture.

There were other times also, at which Mr, Batchel would use the books. Not being a sound sleeper (for book-loving men seldom are), he elected to use as a bedroom one of the two chambers which opened at either side into the library. The arrangement enabled him to beguile many a sleepless hour amongst the books, and in view of these nocturnal visits he kept a candle standing in a sconce above the desk, and matches always ready to his hand.

There was one disadvantage in this close proximity of his bed to the library. Owing, apparently, to some defect in the fittings of the room, which, having no mechanical tastes, Mr Batchel had never investigated, there could be heard, in the stillness of the night, exactly such sounds as might arise from a person moving about amongst the books. Visitors using the other adjacent room would often remark at breakfast, that they had heard their host in the library at one or two o'clock in the morning, when, in fact, he had not left his bed.

Invariably Mr. Batchel allowed them to suppose that he had been where they thought him. He disliked idle controversy, and was unwilling to afford an opening for supernatural talk. Knowing well enough the sounds by which his guests had been deceived, he wanted no other explanation of them than his own, though it was of too vague a character to count as an explanation. He conjectured that the window-sashes, or the doors, or "something," were defective, and was too phlegmatic and too unpractical to make any investigation. The matter gave him no concern.

Persons whose sleep is uncertain are apt to have their worst nights when they would like their best. The consciousness of a special need for rest seems to bring enough mental disturbance to forbid it. So on Christmas Eve, in the year 1907, Mr. Batchel, who would have liked to sleep well, in view of the labours of Christmas Day, lay hopelessly wide awake. He exhausted all the known devices for courting sleep, and, at the end, found himself wider awake than ever. A brilliant moon shone into his room, for he hated window-blinds. There was a light wind blowing, and the sounds in the library were more than usually suggestive of a person moving about. He almost determined to have the sashes "seen to," although he could seldom be induced to have anything "seen to." He disliked changes, even for the better, and would submit to great inconvenience rather than have things altered with which he had become familiar.

As he revolved these matters in his mind, he heard the clocks strike the hour of midnight, and having now lost all hope of falling asleep, he rose from his bed, got into a large dressing gown which hung in readiness for such occasions, and passed into the library, with the intention of reading himself sleepy, if he could.

The moon, by this time, had passed out of the south, and the library seemed all the darker by contrast with the moonlit chamber he had left. He could see nothing but two blue-grey rectangles formed by the windows against the sky, the furniture of the room being altogether invisible. Groping along to where the table stood, Mr. Batchel felt over its surface for the matches which usually lay there; he found, however, that the table was cleared of everything. He raised his right hand, therefore, in order to feel his way to a shelf where the matches were sometimes mislaid, and at that moment, whilst his hand was in mid-air, the matchbox was gently put into it !

Such an incident could hardly fail to disturb even a phlegmatic person, and Mr. Batchel cried "Who's this?" somewhat nervously.

There was no answer. He struck a match, looked hastily round the room, and found it empty, as usual. There was everything, that is to say, that he was accustomed to see, but no other person than himself.

It is not quite accurate, however, to say that everything was in its usual state. Upon the tall desk lay a *quarto* volume that he had certainly not placed there. It was his quite invariable practice to replace his books upon the shelves after using them, and what we may call his library habits were precise and methodical. A book out of place like this, was not only an offence against good order, but a sign that his privacy had been intruded upon. With some surprise, therefore, he lit the candle standing ready in the sconce, and proceeded to examine the book, not sorry, in the disturbed condition in which he was, to have an occupation found for him.

The book proved to be one with which he was unfamiliar,

and this made it certain that some other hand than his had removed it from its place. Its title was *The Compleat Gard'ner* of
M. de la Quintinye made English by John Evelyn Esquire. It was
not a work in which Mr. Batchel felt any great interest. It consisted of divers reflections on various parts of husbandry, doubtless entertaining enough, but too deliberate and discursive for
practical purposes. He had certainly never used the book, and
growing restless now in mind, said to himself that some boy having the freedom of the house, had taken it down from its place
in the hope of finding pictures.

But even whilst he made this explanation he felt its weakness.
To begin with, the desk was too high for a boy. The improbability that any boy would place a book there was equalled by
the improbability that he would leave it there. To discover its
uninviting character would be the work only of a moment, and
no boy would have brought it so far from its shelf.

Mr. Batchel had, however, come to read, and habit was too
strong with him to be wholly set aside. Leaving *The Compleat
Gard'ner* on the desk, he turned round to the shelves to find
some more congenial reading.

Hardly had he done this when he was startled by a sharp
rap upon the desk behind him, followed by a rustling of paper. He turned quickly about and saw the *quarto* lying open.
In obedience to the instinct of the moment, he at once sought
a natural cause for what he saw. Only a wind, and that of the
strongest, could have opened the book, and laid back its heavy
cover; and though he accepted, for a brief moment, that explanation, he was too candid to retain it longer. The wind out of
doors was very light. The window sash was closed and latched,
and, to decide the matter finally, the book had its back, and not
its edges, turned towards the only quarter from which a wind
could strike.

Mr. Batchel approached the desk again and stood over the
book. With increasing perturbation of mind (for he still thought
of the matchbox) he looked upon the open page. Without much
reason beyond that he felt constrained to do something, he read

the words of the half completed sentence at the turn of the page—

at dead of night he left the house and passed into the solitude of the garden.

But he read no more, nor did he give himself the trouble of discovering whose midnight wandering was being described, although the habit was singularly like one of his own. He was in no condition for reading, and turning his back upon the volume he slowly paced the length of the chamber, "wondering at that which had come to pass."

He reached the opposite end of the chamber and was in the act of turning, when again he heard the rustling of paper, and by the time he had faced round, saw the leaves of the book again turning over. In a moment the volume lay at rest, open in another place, and there was no further movement as he approached it. To make sure that he had not been deceived, he read again the words as they entered the page. The author was following a not uncommon practise of the time, and throwing common speech into forms suggested by Holy Writ: "So dig," it said, "that ye may obtain."

This passage, which to Mr. Batchel seemed reprehensible in its levity, excited at once his interest and his disapproval. He was prepared to read more, but this time was not allowed. Before his eye could pass beyond the passage already cited, the leaves of the book slowly turned again, and presented but a termination of five words and a colophon.

The words were, "to the North, an Ilex." These three passages, in which he saw no meaning and no connection, began to entangle themselves together in Mr. Batchel's mind. He found himself repeating them in different orders, now beginning with one, and now with another. Any further attempt at reading he felt to be impossible, and he was in no mind for any more experiences of the unaccountable. Sleep was, of course, further from him than ever, if that were conceivable. What he did, therefore, was to blow out the candle, to return to his moonlit bedroom, and put on more clothing, and then to pass downstairs with the object of going out of doors.

It was not unusual with Mr. Batchel to walk about his garden at night-time. This form of exercise had often, after a wakeful hour, sent him back to his bed refreshed and ready for sleep. The convenient access to the garden at such times lay through his study, whose French windows opened on to a short flight of steps, and upon these he now paused for a moment to admire the snow-like appearance of the lawns, bathed as they were in the moonlight. As he paused, he heard the city clocks strike the half-hour after midnight, and he could not forbear repeating aloud

At dead of night he left the house, and passed into the solitude of the garden.

It was solitary enough. At intervals the screech of an owl, and now and then the noise of a train, seemed to emphasise the solitude by drawing attention to it and then leaving it in possession of the night. Mr. Batchel found himself wondering and conjecturing what Vicar Whitehead, who had acquired the close of land to secure quiet and privacy for garden, would have thought of the railways to the west and north. He turned his face northwards, whence a whistle had just sounded, and saw a tree beautifully outlined against the sky. His breath caught at the sight. Not because the tree was unfamiliar. Mr. Batchel knew all his trees. But what he had seen was "to the north, an *ilex.*"

Mr. Batchel knew not what to make of it all. He had walked into the garden hundreds of times and as often seen the *ilex*, but the words out of the *Compleat Gard'ner* seemed to be pursuing him in a way that made him almost afraid. His temperament, however, as has been said already, was phlegmatic. It was commonly said, and Mr. Batchel approved the verdict, whilst he condemned its inexactness, that "his nerves were made of fiddle-string," so he braced himself afresh and set upon his walk round the silent garden, which he was accustomed to begin in a northerly direction, and was now too proud to change. He usually passed the *ilex* at the beginning of his perambulation, and so would pass it now.

He did not pass it. A small discovery, as he reached it, annoyed and disturbed him. His gardener, as careful and punctilious as himself, never failed to house all his tools at the end of a day's work. Yet there, under the *ilex*, standing upright in moonlight brilliant enough to cast a shadow of it, was a spade.

Mr. Batchel's second thought was one of relief. After his extraordinary experiences in the library (he hardly knew now whether they had been real or not) something quite commonplace would act sedatively, and he determined to carry the spade to the tool-house.

The soil was quite dry, and the surface even a little frozen, so Mr. Batchel left the path, walked up to the spade, and would have drawn it towards him. But it was as if he had made the attempt upon the trunk of the *ilex* itself. The spade would not be moved. Then, first with one hand, and then with both, he tried to raise it, and still it stood firm. Mr. Batchel, of course, attributed this to the frost, slight as it was. Wondering at the spade's being there, and annoyed at its being frozen, he was about to leave it and continue his walk, when the remaining words of the *Compleat Gard'ner* seemed rather to utter themselves, than to await his will—

So dig, that ye may obtain.

Mr. Batchel's power of independent action now deserted him. He took the spade, which no longer resisted, and began to dig. "Five spadefuls and no more," he said aloud. "This is all foolishness."

Four spadefuls of earth he then raised and spread out before him in the moonlight. There was nothing unusual to be seen. Nor did Mr. Batchel decide what he would look for, whether coins, jewels, documents in canisters, or weapons. In point of fact, he dug against what he deemed his better judgment, and expected nothing. He spread before him the fifth and last spadeful of earth, not quite without result, but with no result that was at all sensational. The earth contained a bone. Mr. Batchel's knowledge of anatomy was sufficient to show him that it was a human bone. He identified it, even by moonlight, as the *radius*, a bone of the forearm, as he removed the earth from it, with his thumb.

Such a discovery might be thought worthy of more than the very ordinary interest Mr. Batchel showed. As a matter of fact, the presence of a human bone was easily to be accounted for. Recent excavations within the church had caused the upturning of numberless bones, which had been collected and reverently buried. But an earth-stained bone is also easily overlooked, and this *radius* had obviously found its way into the garden with some of the earth brought out of the church.

Mr. Batchel was glad, rather than regretful at this termination to his adventure. He was once more provided with something to do. The reinterment of such bones as this had been his constant care, and he decided at once to restore the bone to consecrated earth. The time seemed opportune. The eyes of the curious were closed in sleep, he himself was still alert and wakeful. The spade remained by his side and the bone in his hand. So he betook himself, there and then, to the churchyard. By the still generous light of the moon, he found a place where the earth yielded to his spade, and within a few minutes the bone was laid decently to earth, some eighteen inches deep.

The city clocks struck one as he finished. The whole world seemed asleep, and Mr. Batchel slowly returned to the garden with his spade. As he hung it in its accustomed place he felt stealing over him the welcome desire to sleep. He walked quietly on to the house and ascended to his room. It was now dark: the moon had passed on and left the room in shadow. He lit a candle, and before undressing passed into the library. He had an irresistible curiosity to see the passages in John Evelyn's book which had so strangely adapted themselves to the events of the past hour.

In the library a last surprise awaited him. The desk upon which the book had lain was empty. *The Compleat Gard'ner* stood in its place on the shelf. And then Mr. Batchel knew that he had handled a bone of William Whitehead, and that in response to his own entreaty.

The Richpins

Something of the general character of Stoneground and its people has been indicated by stray allusions in the preceding narratives. We must here add that of its present population only a small part is native, the remainder having been attracted during the recent prosperous days of brickmaking, from the nearer parts of East Anglia and the Midlands. The visitor to Stoneground now finds little more than the signs of an unlovely industry, and of the hasty and inadequate housing of the people it has drawn together. Nothing in the place pleases him more than the excellent train-service which makes it easy to get away. He seldom desires a long acquaintance either with Stoneground or its people.

The impression so made upon the average visitor is, however, unjust, as first impressions often are. The few who have made further acquaintance with Stoneground have soon learned to distinguish between the permanent and the accidental features of the place, and have been astonished by nothing so much as by the unexpected evidence of French influence. Amongst the household treasures of the old inhabitants are invariably found French knick-knacks: there are pieces of French furniture in what is called "the room" of many houses. A certain ten-acre field is called the "Frenchman's meadow." Upon the voters' lists hanging at the church door are to be found French names, often corrupted; and boys who run about the streets can be heard shrieking to each other such names as Bunnum, Dangibow, Planchey, and so on.

Mr. Batchel himself is possessed of many curious little articles of French handiwork—boxes deftly covered with split straws, arranged ingeniously in patterns; models of the guillotine, built of carved meat-bones, and various other pieces of handiwork, amongst them an accurate road-map of the country between Stoneground and Yarmouth, drawn upon a fly-leaf torn from some book, and bearing upon the other side the name of Jules Richepin, The latter had been picked up, according to a pencil-led-note written across one corner, by a shepherd, in the year 1811.

The explanation of this French influence is simple enough. Within five miles of Stoneground a large barracks had been erected for the custody of French prisoners during the war with Bonaparte. Many thousands were confined there during the years 1808—14. The prisoners were allowed to sell what articles they could make in the barracks; and many of them, upon their release, settled in the neighbourhood, where their descendants remain. There is little curiosity amongst these descendants about their origin. The events of a century ago seem to them as re-mote as the Deluge, and as immaterial.

To Thomas Richpin, a weakly man who blew the organ in church, Mr. Batchel shewed the map. Richpin, with a broad, black-haired skull and a narrow chin which grew a little pointed beard, had always a foreign look about him: Mr. Batchel thought it more than possible that he might be descended from the owner of the book, and told him as much upon shewing him the fly-leaf. Thomas, however, was content to observe that "his name hadn't got no E," and shewed no further interest in the matter. His interest in it, before we have done with him, will have become very large.

For the growing boys of Stoneground, with whom he was on generally friendly terms, Mr. Batchel formed certain clubs to provide them with occupation on winter evenings; and in these clubs, in the interests of peace and good order, he spent a great deal of time. Sitting one December evening, in a large circle of boys who preferred the warmth of the fire to the more temperate atmosphere of the tables, he found Thomas Richpin the sole topic of conversation.

"We seen Mr. Richpin in Frenchman's Meadow last night," said one.

"What time?" said Mr. Batchel, whose function it was to act as a sort of fly-wheel, and to carry the conversation over dead points. He had received the information with some little surprise, because Frenchman's Meadow was an unusual place for Richpin to have been in, but his question had no further object than to encourage talk.

"Half-past nine," was the reply.

This made the question much more interesting. Mr. Batchel, on the preceding evening, had taken advantage of a warmed church to practise upon the organ. He had played it from nine o'clock until ten, and Richpin had been all that time at the bellows.

"Are you sure it was half-past nine?" he asked.

"Yes," (we reproduce the answer exactly), "we come out o' night-school at quarter-past, and we was all goin' to the Wash to look if it was friz."

"And you saw Mr. Richpin in Frenchman's Meadow?" said Mr. Batchel.

"Yes. He was looking for something on the ground," added another boy.

"And his trousers was tore," said a third.

The story was clearly destined to stand in no need of corroboration.

"Did Mr. Richpin speak to you?" enquired Mr. Batchel.

"No, we run away afore he come to us," was the answer.

"Why?"

"Because we was frit."

"What frightened you?"

"Jim Lallement hauled a flint at him and hit him in the face, and he didn't take no notice, so we run away."

"Why?" repeated Mr. Batchel.

"Because he never hollered nor looked at us, and it made us

33

feel so funny."

"Did you go straight down to the Wash?"

They had all done so.

"What time was it when you reached home?"

They had all been at home by ten, before Richpin had left the church.

"Why do they call it Frenchman's Meadow?" asked another boy, evidently anxious to change the subject.

Mr. Batchel replied that the meadow had probably belonged to a Frenchman whose name was not easy to say, and the conversation after this was soon in another channel. But, furnished as he was with an unmistakeable alibi, the story about Richpin and the torn trousers, and the flint, greatly puzzled him.

"Go straight home," he said, as the boys at last bade him goodnight, "and let us have no more stone-throwing." They were reckless boys, and Richpin, who used little discretion in reporting their misdemeanours about the church, seemed to Mr. Satchel to stand in real danger.

Frenchman's Meadow provided ten acres of excellent pasture, and the owners of two or three hard-worked horses were glad to pay three shillings a week for the privilege of turning them into it. One of these men came to Mr. Batchel on the morning which followed the conversation at the club.

"I'm in a bit of a quandary about Tom Richpin," he began.

This was an opening that did not fail to command Mr. Batchel's attention. "What is it?" he said.

"I had my mare in Frenchman's Meadow," replied the man, "and Sam Bower come and told me last night as he heard her gallopin' about when he was walking this side the hedge."

"But what about Richpin?" said Mr. Batchel.

"Let me come to it," said the other. "My mare hasn't got no wind to gallop, so I up and went to see to her, and there she was sure enough, like a wild thing, and Tom Richpin walking across the meadow."

"Was he chasing her?" asked Mr. Batchel, who felt the absurdity of the question as he put it.

"He was not," said the man, "but what he could have been doin' to put the mare into that state, I can't think."

"What was he doing when you saw him?" asked Mr. Batchel.

"He was walking along looking for something he'd dropped, with his trousers all tore to ribbons, and while I was catchin' the mare, he made off."

"He was easy enough to find, I suppose?" said Mr. Batchel.

"That's the quandary I was put in," said the man. "I took the mare home and gave her to my lad, and straight I went to Richpin's, and found Tom havin' his supper, with his trousers as good as new."

"You'd made a mistake," said Mr. Batchel.

"But how come the mare to make it too?" said the other.

"What did you say to Richpin?" asked Mr. Batchel.

"Tom," I says, "when did you come in? 'Six o'clock,' he says, 'I bin mendin' my boots'; and there, sure enough, was the bobbin' iron by his chair, and him in his stockin' feet. I don't know what to do."

"Give the mare a rest," said Mr. Batchel, "and say no more about it."

"I don't want to harm a pore creature like Richpin," said the man, "but a mare's a mare, especially where there's a family to bring up." The man consented, however, to abide by Mr. Batchel's advice, and the interview ended. The evenings just then were light, and both the man and his mare had seen something for which Mr. Batchel could not, at present, account. The worst way, however, of arriving at an explanation is to guess it. He was far too wise to let himself wander into the pleasant fields of conjecture, and had determined, even before the story of the mare had finished, upon the more prosaic path of investigation.

Mr. Batchel, either from strength or indolence of mind, as the reader may be pleased to determine, did not allow matters even of this exciting kind, to disturb his daily round of duty. He was beginning to fear, after what he had heard of the Frenchman's Meadow, that he might find it necessary to preach a plain sermon upon the Witch of Endor, for he foresaw that there would soon be some ghostly talk in circulation. In small communities, like that of Stoneground, such talk arises upon very slight provocation, and here was nothing at all to check it. Richpin was a weak and timid man, whom no one would suspect, whilst an alternative remained open, of wandering about in the dark; and Mr. Batchel knew that the alternative of an apparition, if once suggested, would meet with general acceptance, and this he wished, at all costs, to avoid. His own view of the matter he held in reserve, for the reasons already stated, but he could not help suspecting that there might be a better explanation of the name "Frenchman's Meadow" than he had given to the boys at their club.

Afternoons, with Mr. Batchel, were always spent in making pastoral visits, and upon the day our story has reached he determined to include amongst them a call upon Richpin, and to submit him to a cautious cross-examination. It was evident that at least four persons, all perfectly familiar with his appearance, were under the impression that they had seen him in the meadow, and his own statement upon the matter would be at least worth hearing.

Richpin's home, however, was not the first one visited by Mr. Batchel on that afternoon. His friendly relations with the boys has already been mentioned, and it may now be added that this friendship was but part of a generally keen sympathy with young people of all ages, and of both sexes. Parents knew much less than he did of the love affairs of their young people; and if he was not actually guilty of match-making, he was at least a very sympathetic observer of the process. When lovers had their little differences, or even their greater ones, it was Mr. Batchel, in most cases, who adjusted them, and who suffered, if he failed, hardly less than the lovers themselves.

It was a negotiation of this kind which, on this particular day, had given precedence to another visit, and left Richpin until the later part of the afternoon. But the matter of the Frenchman's Meadow had, after all, not to wait for Richpin. Mr. Batchel was calculating how long he should be in reaching it, when he found himself unexpectedly there. Selina Broughton had been a favourite of his from her childhood; she had been sufficiently good to please him, and naughty enough to attract and challenge him; and when at length she began to walk out with Bob Rock-fort, who was another favourite, Mr. Batchel rubbed his hands in satisfaction. Their present difference, which now brought him to the Broughtons' cottage, gave him but little anxiety. He had brought Bob half-way towards reconciliation, and had no doubt of his ability to lead Selina to the same place. They would finish the journey, happily enough, together.

But what has this to do with the Frenchman's Meadow? Much every way. The meadow was apt to be the rendezvous of such young people as desired a higher degree of privacy than that afforded by the public paths; and these two had gone there separately the night before, each to nurse a grievance against the other. They had been at opposite ends, as it chanced, of the field; and Bob, who believed himself to be alone there, had been awakened from his reverie by a sudden scream.

He had at once run across the field, and found Selina sorely in need of him. Mr. Batchel's work of reconciliation had been there and then anticipated, and Bob had taken the girl home in a condition of great excitement to her mother. All this was explained, in breathless sentences, by Mrs. Broughton, by way of accounting for the fact that Selina was then lying down in "the room."

There was no reason why Mr. Batchel should not see her, of course, and he went in. His original errand had lapsed, but it was now replaced by one of greater interest. Evidently there was Selina's testimony to add to that of the other four; she was not a girl who would scream without good cause, and Mr. Batchel felt that he knew how his question about the cause would be answered, when he came to the point of asking it.

He was not quite prepared for the form of her answer, which she gave without any hesitation. She had seen Mr. Richpin "looking for his eyes." Mr. Batchel saved for another occasion the amusement to be derived from the curiously illogical answer. He saw at once what had suggested it. Richpin had until recently had an atrocious squint, which an operation in London had completely cured. This operation, of which, of course, he knew nothing, he had described, in his own way, to anyone who would listen, and it was commonly believed that his eyes had ceased to be fixtures.

It was plain, however, that Selina had seen very much what had been seen by the other four. Her information was precise, and her story perfectly coherent. She preserved a maidenly reticence about his trousers, if she had noticed them; but added a new fact, and a terrible one, in her description of the eyeless sockets. No wonder she had screamed. It will be observed that Mr. Richpin was still searching, if not looking, for something upon the ground.

Mr. Batchel now proceeded to make his remaining visit. Richpin lived in a little cottage by the church, of which cottage the Vicar was the indulgent landlord. Richpin's creditors were obliged to shew some indulgence, because his income was never regular and seldom sufficient. He got on in life by what is called "rubbing along," and appeared to do it with surprisingly little friction. The small duties about the church, assigned to him out of charity, were overpaid. He succeeded in attracting to himself all the available gifts of masculine clothing, of which he probably received enough and to sell, and he had somehow wooed and won a capable, if not very comely, wife, who supplemented his income by her own labour, and managed her house and husband to admiration.

Richpin, however, was not by any means a mere dependent upon charity. He was, in his way, a man of parts. All plants, for instance, were his friends, and he had inherited, or acquired, great skill with fruit-trees, which never failed to reward his treatment with abundant crops. The two or three vines, too, of the neighbourhood, he kept in fine order by methods of his own, whose merit was proved by their success. He had other skill, though of a less remunerative kind, in fashioning toys out of wood, cardboard, or paper; and every correctly-behaving child in the parish had some such product of his handiwork.

And besides all this, Richpin had a remarkable aptitude for making music. He could do something upon every musical instrument that came in his way, and, but for his voice, which was like that of the peahen, would have been a singer. It was his voice that had secured him the situation of organ-blower, as one remote from all incitement to join in the singing in church.

Like all men who have not wit enough to defend themselves by argument, Richpin had a plaintive manner. His way of resenting injury was to complain of it to the next person he met, and such complaints as he found no other means of discharging, he carried home to his wife, who treated his conversation just as she treated the singing of the canary, and other domestic sounds, being hardly conscious of it until it ceased.

The entrance of Mr. Batchel, soon after his interview with Selina, found Richpin engaged in a loud and fluent oration. The fluency was achieved mainly by repetition, for the man had but small command of words, but it served none the less to shew the depth of his indignation.

"I aren't bin in Frenchman's Meadow, am I?" he was saying in appeal to his wife—this is the Stoneground way with auxiliary verbs—"What am I got to go there for?" He acknowledged Mr. Batchel's entrance in no other way than by changing to the third person in his discourse, and he continued without pause—"if she'd let me out o' nights, I'm got better places to go to than Frenchman's Meadow. Let policeman stick to where I am bin, or else keep his mouth shut. What call is he got to say I'm bin where I aren't bin?"

From this, and much more to the same effect, it was clear that the matter of the meadow was being noised abroad, and even receiving official attention. Mr. Batchel was well aware that no question he could put to Richpin, in his present state, would change the flow of his eloquence, and that he had already learned as much as he was likely to learn. He was content, therefore, to ascertain from Mrs. Richpin that her husband had indeed spent all his evenings at home, with the single exception of the one hour during which Mr. Batchel had employed him at the organ. Having ascertained this, he retired, and left Richpin to talk himself out.

No further doubt about the story was now possible. It was not twenty-four hours since Mr. Batchel had heard it from the boys at the club, and it had already been confirmed by at least two unimpeachable witnesses. He thought the matter over, as he took his tea, and was chiefly concerned in Richpin's curious connexion with it. On his account, more than on any other, it had become necessary to make whatever investigation might be feasible, and Mr. Batchel determined, of course, to make the next stage of it in the meadow itself.

The situation of "Frenchman's Meadow" made it more con-spicuous than any other enclosure in the neighbourhood. It was upon the edge of what is locally known as "high land"; and though its elevation was not great, one could stand in the mead-ow and look seawards over many miles of flat country, once a waste of brackish water, now a great chess-board of fertile fields bounded by straight dykes of glistening water. The point of view derived another interest from looking down upon a long straight bank which disappeared into the horizon many miles away, and might have been taken for a great railway em-bankment of which no use had been made.

It was, in fact, one of the great works of the Dutch engineers in the time of Charles I., and it separated the river basin from a large drained area called the "Middle Level," some six feet below it. In this embankment, not two hundred yards below "French-man's Meadow," was one of the huge water gates which admit-ted traffic through a sluice, into the lower level, and the pictur-esque thatched cottage of the sluice-keeper formed a pleasing addition to the landscape.

It was a view with which Mr. Batchel was naturally very familiar. Few of his surroundings were pleasant to the eye, and this was about the only place to which he could take a visitor whom he desired to impress favourably. The way to the meadow lay through a short lane, and he could reach it in five minutes: he was frequently there.

It was, of course, his intention to be there again that evening: to spend the night there, if need be, rather than let anything escape him. He only hoped he should not find half the parish there also. His best hope of privacy lay in the inclemency of the weather; the day was growing colder, and there was a north-east wind, of which Frenchman's Meadow would receive the fine edge.

Mr. Batchel spent the next three hours in dealing with some arrears of correspondence, and at nine o'clock put on his thickest coat and boots, and made his way to the meadow. It became evident, as he walked up the lane, that he was to have company. He heard many voices, and soon recognised the loudest amongst them. Jim Lallement was boasting of the accuracy of his aim: the others were not disputing it, but were asserting their own merits in discordant chorus. This was a nuisance, and to make matters worse, Mr. Batchel heard steps behind him.

A voice soon bade him "Good evening." To Mr. Batchel's great relief it proved to be the policeman, who soon overtook him. The conversation began on his side.

"Curious tricks, sir, these of Richpin's."

"What tricks?" asked Mr. Batchel, with an air of innocence.

"Why, he's been walking about Frenchman's Meadow these three nights, frightening folk and what all."

"Richpin has been at home every night, and all night long," said Mr. Batchel.

"I'm talking about where he was, not where he says he was," said the policeman. "You can't go behind the evidence."

"But Richpin has evidence too. I asked his wife."

"You know, sir, and none better, that wives have got to obey. Richpin wants to be took for a ghost, and we know that sort of ghost. Whenever we hear there's a ghost, we always know there's going to be turkeys missing."

"But there are real ghosts sometimes, surely?" said Mr. Batchel.

41

"No," said the policeman, "me and my wife have both looked, and there's no such thing."

"Looked where?" enquired Mr. Batchel.

"In the 'Police Duty' catechism. There's lunatics, and deserters, and dead bodies, but no ghosts."

Mr. Batchel accepted this as final. He had devised a way of ridding himself of all his company, and proceeded at once to carry it into effect. The two had by this time reached the group of boys.

"These are all stone-throwers," said he, loudly.

There was a clatter of stones as they dropped from the hands of the boys.

"These boys ought all to be in the club instead of roaming about here damaging property. Will you take them there, and see them safely in? If Richpin comes here, I will bring him to the station."

The policeman seemed well pleased with the suggestion. No doubt he had overstated his confidence in the definition of the "Police Duty." Mr. Batchel, on his part, knew the boys well enough to be assured that they would keep the policeman occupied for the next half-hour, and as the party moved slowly away, felt proud of his diplomacy.

There was no sign of any other person about the field gate, which he climbed readily enough, and he was soon standing in the highest part of the meadow and peering into the darkness on every side.

It was possible to see a distance of about thirty yards; beyond that it was too dark to distinguish anything. Mr. Batchel designed a zigzag course about the meadow, which would allow of his examining it systematically and as rapidly as possible, and along this course he began to walk briskly, looking straight before him as he went, and pausing to look well about him when he came to a turn. There were no beasts in the meadow—their owners had taken the precaution of removing them; their absence was, of course, of great advantage to Mr. Batchel.

In about ten minutes he had finished his zigzag path and arrived at the other corner of the meadow; he had seen nothing resembling a man. He then retraced his steps, and examined the field again, but arrived at his starting point, knowing no more than when he had left it. He began to fear the return of the policeman as he faced the wind and set upon a third journey.

The third journey, however, rewarded him. He had reached the end of his second traverse, and was looking about him at the angle between that and the next, when he distinctly saw what looked like Richpin crossing his circle of vision, and making straight for the sluice. There was no gate on that side of the field; the hedge, which seemed to present no obstacle to the other, delayed Mr. Batchel considerably, and still retains some of his clothing, but he was not long through before he had again marked his man. It had every appearance of being Richpin. It went down the slope, crossed the plank that bridged the lock, and disappeared round the corner of the cottage, where the entrance lay.

Mr. Batchel had had no opportunity of confirming the gruesome observation of Selina Broughton, but had seen enough to prove that the others had not been romancing. He was not a half-minute behind the figure as it crossed the plank over the lock—it was slow going in the darkness—and he followed it immediately round the corner of the house. As he expected, it had then disappeared.

Mr. Batchel knocked at the door, and admitted himself, as his custom was. The sluice-keeper was in his kitchen, charring a gate post. He was surprised to see Mr. Batchel at that hour, and his greeting took the form of a remark to that effect.

"I have been taking an evening walk," said Mr. Batchel. "Have you seen Richpin lately?"

"I see him last Saturday week," replied the sluice-keeper, "not since."

"Do you feel lonely here at night?"

"No," replied the sluice-keeper, "people drop in at times. There was a man in on Monday, and another yesterday."

"Have you had no one today?" said Mr. Batchel, coming to

the point.

The answer showed that Mr. Batchel had been the first to enter the door that day, and after a little general conversation he brought his visit to an end.

It was now ten o'clock. He looked in at Richpin's cottage, where he saw a light burning, as he passed. Richpin had tired himself early, and had been in bed since half-past eight. His wife was visibly annoyed at the rumours which had upset him, and Mr. Batchel said such soothing words as he could command, before he left for home.

He congratulated himself, prematurely, as he sat before the fire in his study, that the day was at an end. It had been cold out of doors, and it was pleasant to think things over in the warmth of the cheerful fire his housekeeper never failed to leave for him. The reader will have no more difficulty than Mr. Batchel had in accounting for the resemblance between Richpin and the man in the meadow. It was a mere question of family likeness. That the ancestor had been seen in the meadow at some former time might perhaps be inferred from its traditional name. The reason for his return, then and now, was a matter of mere conjecture, and Mr. Batchel let it alone.

The next incident has, to some, appeared incredible, which only means, after all, that it has made demands upon their powers of imagination and found them bankrupt.

Critics of story-telling have used severe language about authors who avail themselves of the shortcut of coincidence. "That must be reserved, I suppose," said Mr. Batchel, when he came to tell of Richpin, "for what really happens; and that fiction is a game which must be played according to the rules."

"I know," he went on to say, "that the chances were some millions to one against what happened that night, but if that makes it incredible, what is there left to believe?"

It was thereupon remarked by someone in the company, that the credible material would not be exhausted.

"I doubt whether anything happens," replied Mr. Batchel in his dogmatic way, "without the chances being a million to one against it. Why did they choose such a word? What does 'happen' mean?"

There was no reply: it was clearly a rhetorical question.

"Is it incredible," he went on, "that I put into the plate last Sunday the very half-crown my uncle tipped me with in 1881, and that I spent next day?"

"Was that the one you put in?" was asked by several.

"How do I know?" replied Mr. Batchel, "but if I knew the history of the half-crown I did put in, I know it would furnish still more remarkable coincidences."

All this talk arose out of the fact that at midnight on the eventful day, whilst Mr. Batchel was still sitting by his study fire, he had news that the cottage at the sluice had been burnt down. The thatch had been dry; there was, as we know, a stiff east-wind, and an hour had sufficed to destroy all that was inflammable. The fire is still spoken of in Stoneground with great regret. There remains only one building in the place of sufficient merit to find its way on to a postcard.

It was just at midnight that the sluice-keeper rung at Mr. Batchel's door. His errand required no apology. The man had found a night-fisherman to help him as soon as the fire began, and with two long sprits from a lighter they had made haste to tear down the thatch, and upon this had brought down, from under the ridge at the south end, the bones and some of the clothing of a man. Would Mr. Batchel come down and see?

Mr. Batchel put on his coat and returned to the place. The people whom the fire had collected had been kept on the further side of the water, and the space about the cottage was vacant. Near to the smouldering heap of ruin were the remains found under the thatch. The fingers of the right hand still firmly clutched a sheep bone which had been gnawed as a dog would gnaw it.

"Starved to death," said the sluice-keeper, "I see a tramp like that ten years ago."

They laid the bones decently in an outhouse, and turned the key, Mr. Batchel carried home in his hand a metal cross, threaded

45

upon a cord. He found an engraved figure of Our Lord on the face of it, and the name of Pierre Richepin upon the back. He went next day to make the matter known to the nearest Priest of the Roman Faith, with whom he left the cross. The remains, after a brief inquest, were interred in the cemetery, with the rites of the church to which the man had evidently belonged.

Mr. Batchel's deductions from the whole circumstances were curious, and left a great deal to be explained. It seemed as if Pierre Richepin had been disturbed by some premonition of the fire, but had not foreseen that his mortal remains would escape; that he could not return to his own people without the aid of his map, but had no perception of the interval that had elapsed since he had lost it. This map Mr. Batchel put into his pocket-book next day when he went to Thomas Richpin for certain other information about his surviving relatives.

Richpin had a father, it appeared, living a few miles away in Jakesley Fen, and Mr. Batchel concluded that he was worth a visit. He mounted his bicycle, therefore, and made his way to Jakesley that same afternoon.

Mr. Richpin was working not far from home, and was soon brought in. He and his wife shewed great courtesy to their visitor, whom they knew well by repute. They had a well-ordered house, and with a natural and dignified hospitality, asked him to take tea with them. It was evident to Mr. Batchel that there was a great gulf between the elder Richpin and his son; the former was the last of an old race, and the latter the first of a new. In spite of the Board of Education, the latter was vastly the worse.

The cottage contained some French *kickshaws* which greatly facilitated the enquiries Mr. Batchel had come to make. They proved to be family relics.

"My grandfather," said Mr. Richpin, as they sat at tea, "was a prisoner—he and his brother."

"Your grandfather was Pierre Richepin? "asked Mr. Batchel.

"No! Jules," was the reply. "Pierre got away."

"Shew Mr. Batchel the book," said his wife.

The book was produced. It was a *Book of Meditations*, with

the name of Jules Richepin upon the title-page. The fly-leaf was missing. Mr. Batchel produced the map from his pocket-book. It fitted exactly. The slight indentures along the torn edge fell into their place, and Mr. Batchel left the leaf in the book, to the great delight of the old couple, to whom he told no more of the story than he thought fit.

The Eastern Window

It may well be that Vermuyden and the Dutchmen who drained the fens did good, and that it was interred with their bones. It is quite certain that they did evil and that it lives after them. The rivers, which these men robbed of their water, have at length silted up, and the drainage of one tract of country is proving to have been achieved by the undraining of another.

Places like Stoneground, which lie on the banks of these defrauded rivers, are now become helpless victims of Dutch engineering. The water which has lost its natural outlet, invades their lands. The thrifty cottager who once had the river at the bottom of his garden, has his garden more often in these days, at the bottom of the river, and a summer flood not infrequently destroys the whole produce of his ground.

Such a flood, during an early year in the 20th century, had been unusually disastrous to Stoneground, and Mr. Batchel, who, as a gardener, was well able to estimate the losses of his poorer neighbours, was taking some steps towards repairing them.

Money, however, is never at rest in Stoneground, and it turned out upon this occasion that the funds placed at his command were wholly inadequate to the charitable purpose assigned to them. It seemed as if those who had lost a rood of potatoes could be compensated for no more than a yard.

It was at this time, when he was oppressed in mind by the failure of his charitable enterprise, that Mr. Batchel met with the happy adventure in which the eastern window of the church played so singular a part.

The narrative should be prefaced by a brief description of the window in question. It is a large painted window, of a somewhat unfortunate period of execution. The drawing and colouring leave everything to be desired. The scheme of the window, however, is based upon a wholesome tradition. The five large lights in the lower part are assigned to five scenes in the life of Our Lord, and the second of these, counting from the North, contains a bold erect figure of St. John Baptist, to whom the church is dedicated. It is this figure alone, of all those contained in the window, that is concerned in what we have to relate.

It has already been mentioned that Mr. Batchel had some knowledge of music. He took an interest in the choir, from whose practices he was seldom absent; and was quite competent, in the occasional absence of the choirmaster, to act as his deputy. It is customary at Stoneground for the choirmaster, in order to save the sexton a journey, to extinguish the lights after a choir-practice and to lock up the church. These duties, accordingly, were performed by Mr. Batchel when the need arose.

It will be of use to the reader to have the procedure in detail. The large gas-meter stood in an aisle of the church, and it was Mr. Batchel's practice to go round and extinguish all the lights save one, before turning off the gas at the meter. The one remaining light, which was reached by standing upon a choir seat, was always that nearest the door of the chancel, and experience proved that there was ample time to walk from the meter to that light before it died out. It was therefore an easy matter to turn of the last light, to find the door without its aid, and thence to pass out, and close the church for the night.

Upon the evening of which we have to speak, the choir had hurried out as usual, as soon as the word had been given. Mr. Batchel had remained to gather together some of the books they had left in disorder, and then turned out the lights in the manner already described. But as soon as he had extinguished the last light, his eye fell, as he descended carefully from the seat, upon the figure of the Baptist. There was just enough light outside to make the figures visible in the Eastern Window, and Mr. Batchel saw the figure of St. John raise the right arm to its full extent, and point northward, turning its head, at the same time, so as to look him full in the face. These movements were three times repeated, and, after that, the figure came to rest in its normal and familiar position.

The reader will not suppose, any more than Mr. Batchel supposed, that a figure painted upon glass had suddenly been endowed with the power of movement. But that there had been the appearance of movement admitted of no doubt, and Mr. Batchel was not so incurious as to let the matter pass without some attempt at investigation. It must be remembered, too, that an experience in the old library, which has been previously recorded, had predisposed him to give attention to signs which another man might have wished to explain away.

He was not willing, therefore, to leave this matter where it stood. He was quite prepared to think that his eye had been deceived, but was none the less determined to find out what had deceived it. One thing he had no difficulty in deciding. If the movement had not been actually within the Baptist's figure, it had been immediately behind it. Without delay, therefore, he passed out of the church and locked the door after him, with the intention of examining the other side of the window.

Every inhabitant of Stoneground knows, and laments, the ruin of the old manor house. Its loss by fire some fifteen years ago was a calamity from which the parish has never recovered. The estate was acquired, soon after the destruction of the house, by speculators who have been unable to turn it to any account, and it has for a decade or longer been "let alone," except by the forces of nature and the wantonness of trespassers. The charred remains of the house still project above the surrounding heaps of fallen masonry, which have long been overgrown by such vegetation as thrives on neglected ground; and what was once a stately house, with its garden and park in fine order, has given place to a scene of desolation and ruin.

Stoneground church was built, some 600 years ago, within the enclosure of the Manor House, or, as it was anciently termed, the Burystead, and an excellent stratum of gravel such as no builder would wisely disregard, brought the house and church unusually near together. In more primitive days, the nearness probably caused no inconvenience; but when change and progress affected the popular idea of respectful distance, the churchyard came to be separated by a substantial stone wall, of sufficient height to secure the privacy of the house.

The change was made with necessary regard to economy of space. The eastern wall of the church already projected far into the garden of the manor, and lay but fifty yards from the south front of the house. On that side of the churchyard, therefore, the new wall was set back. Running from the north to the nearest corner of the church, it was there built up to the church itself, and then continued from the southern corner, leaving the eastern wall and window within the garden of the squire. It was his ivy that clung to the wall of the church, and his trees that shaded the window from the morning sun.

Whilst we have been recalling these facts, Mr. Batchel has made his way out of the church and through the churchyard, and has arrived at a small door in the boundary wall, close to the S. E. corner of the chancel. It was a door which some squire of the previous century had made, to give convenient access to the church for himself and his household. It has no present use, and Mr. Batchel had some difficulty in getting it open. It was not long, however, before he stood on the inner side, and was examining the second light of the window. There was a tolerably bright moon, and the dark surface of the glass could be distinctly seen, as well as the wirework placed there for its protection.

A tall birch, one of the trees of the old churchyard, had thrust its lower boughs across the window, and their silvery bark shone in the moonlight. The boughs were bare of leaves, and only very slightly interrupted Mr. Batchel's view of the Baptist's figure, the leaden outline of which was clearly traceable. There was nothing, however, to account for the movement which Mr. Batchel was curious to investigate.

He was about to turn homewards in some disappointment,

when a cloud obscured the moon again, and reduced the light to what it had been before he left the church. Mr. Batchel watched the darkening of the window and the objects near it, and as the figure of the Baptist disappeared from view there came into sight a creamy vaporous figure of another person lightly poised upon the bough of the tree, and almost coincident in position with the picture of the Saint.

It could hardly be described as the figure of a person. It had more the appearance of half a person, and fancifully suggested to Mr. Batchel, who was fond of whist, one of the diagonally bisected knaves in a pack of cards, as he appears when another card conceals a triangular half of the bust.

There was no question, now, of going home. Mr. Batchel's eyes were riveted upon the apparition. It disappeared again for a moment, when an interval between two clouds restored the light of the moon; but no sooner had the second cloud replaced the first than the figure again became distinct. And upon this, its single arm was raised three times, pointing northwards towards the ruined house, just as the figure of the Baptist had seemed to point when Mr. Batchel had seen it from within the church.

It was natural that upon receipt of this sign Mr. Batchel should step nearer to the tree, from which he was still at some little distance, and as he moved, the figure floated obliquely downwards and came to rest in a direct line between him and the ruins of the house. It rested, not upon the ground, but in just such a position as it would have occupied if the lower parts had been there, and in this position it seemed to await Mr. Batchel's advance. He made such haste to approach it as was possible upon ground encumbered with ivy and brambles, and the figure responded to every advance of his by moving further in the direction of the ruin.

As the ground improved, the progress became more rapid. Soon they were both upon an open stretch of grass, which in better days had been a lawn, and still the figure retreated towards the building, with Mr. Batchel in respectful pursuit. He saw it, at last, poised upon the summit of a heap of masonry, and it disappeared, at his near approach, into a crevice between two large stones.

The timely reappearance of the moon just enabled Mr. Batchel to perceive this crevice, and he took advantage of the interval of light to mark the place. Taking up a large twig that lay at his feet, he inserted it between the stones. He made a slit in the free end and drew into it one of some papers that he had carried out of the church. After such a precaution it could hardly be possible to lose the place—for, of course, Mr. Batchel intended to return in daylight and continue his investigation. For the present, it seemed to be at an end. The light was soon obscured again, but there was no reappearance of the singular figure he had followed, so after remaining about the spot for a few minutes, Mr. Batchel went home to his customary occupation.

He was not a man to let these occupations be disturbed even by a somewhat exciting adventure, nor was he one of those who regard an unusual experience only as a sign of nervous disorder. Mr. Batchel had far too broad a mind to discredit his sensations because they were not like those of other people. Even had his adventure of the evening been shared by some companion who saw less than he did, Mr. Batchel would only have inferred that his own part in the matter was being regarded as more important.

Next morning, therefore, he lost no time in returning to the scene of his adventure. He found his mark undisturbed, and was able to examine the crevice into which the apparition had seemed to enter. It was a crevice formed by the curved surfaces of two large stones which lay together on the top of a small heap of fallen rubbish, and these two stones Mr. Batchel proceeded to remove. His strength was just sufficient for the purpose. He laid the stones upon the ground on either side of the little mound, and then proceeded to remove, with his hands, the rubbish upon which they had rested, and amongst the rubbish he found, tarnished and blackened, two silver coins.

It was not a discovery which seemed to afford any explanation of what had occurred the night before, but Mr. Batchel could not but suppose that there had been an attempt to direct his attention to the coins, and he carried them away with a view of submitting them to a careful examination. Taking them up to his bedroom he poured a little water into a hand basin, and soon succeeded, with the aid of soap and a nail brush, in making them tolerably clean. Ten minutes later, after adding ammonia to the water, he had made them bright, and after carefully drying them, was able to make his examination.

They were two crowns of the time of Queen Anne, minted, as a small letter E indicated, at Edinburgh, and stamped with the roses and plumes which testified to the English and Welsh silver in their composition. The coins bore no date, but Mr. Batchel had no hesitation in assigning them to the year 1708 or thereabouts. They were handsome coins, and in themselves a find of considerable interest, but there was nothing to show why he had been directed to their place of concealment. It was an enigma, and he could not solve it. He had other work to do, so he laid the two crowns upon his dressing table, and proceeded to do it.

Mr. Batchel thought little more of the coins until bedtime, when he took them from the table and bestowed upon them another admiring examination by the light of his candle. But the examination told him nothing new: he laid them down again, and, before very long, had lain his own head upon the pillow.

It was Mr. Batchel's custom to read himself to sleep. At this time he happened to be re-reading the Waverley novels, and *Woodstock* lay upon the reading-stand which was always placed at his bedside. As he read of the cleverly devised apparition at Woodstock, he naturally asked himself whether he might not have been the victim of some similar trickery, but was not long in coming to the conclusion that his experience admitted of no such explanation. He soon dismissed the matter from his mind and went on with his book.

On this occasion, however, he was tired of reading before he was ready for sleep; it was long in coming, and then did not come to stay. His rest, in fact, was greatly disturbed. Again and again, perhaps every hour or so, he was awakened by an uneasy consciousness of some other presence in the room.

Upon one of his later awakenings, he was distinctly sensible of a sound, or what he described to himself as the "ghost" of a sound.

He compared it to the whining of a dog that had lost its voice. It was not a very intelligible comparison, but still it seemed to describe his sensation. The sound, if we may so call it caused him first to sit up in bed and look well about him, and then, when nothing had come of that, to light his candle. It was not to be expected that anything should come of that, but it had seemed a comfortable thing to do, and Mr. Batchel left the candle alight and read his book for half an hour or so, before blowing it out.

After this, there was no further interruption, but Mr. Batchel distinctly felt, when it was time to leave his bed, that he had had a bad night. The coins, almost to his surprise, lay undisturbed. He went to ascertain this as soon as he was on his feet. He would almost have welcomed their removal, or at any rate, some change which might have helped him towards a theory of his adventure. There was, however, nothing. If he had, in fact, been visited during the night, the coins would seem to have had nothing to do with the matter.

Mr. Batchel left the two crowns lying on his table on this next day, and went about his ordinary duties. They were such duties as afforded full occupation for his mind, and he gave no more than a passing thought to the coins, until he was again retiring to rest. He had certainly intended to return to the heap of rubbish from which he had taken them, but had not found leisure to do so. He did not handle the coins again. As he undressed, he made some attempt to estimate their value, but without having arrived at any conclusion, went on to think of other things, and in a little while had lain down to rest again, hoping for a better night.

His hopes were disappointed. Within an hour of falling asleep he found himself awakened again by the voiceless whining he so well remembered. This sound, as for convenience we will call it, was now persistent and continuous. Mr. Batchel gave up even trying to sleep, and as he grew more restless and uneasy, decided to get up and dress.

It was the entire cessation of the sound at this juncture which led him to a suspicion. His rising was evidently giving satisfaction. From that it was easy to infer that something had been desired of him, both on the present and the preceding night. Mr. Batchel was not one to hold himself aloof in such a case. If help was wanted, even in such unnatural circumstances, he was ready to offer it. He determined, accordingly, to return to the manor house, and when he had finished dressing, descended the stairs, put on a warm overcoat and went out, closing his hall door behind him, without having heard any more of the sound, either whilst dressing, or whilst leaving the house.

Once out of doors, the suspicion he had formed was strengthened into a conviction. There was no manner of doubt that he had been fetched from his bed; for about thirty yards in front of him he saw the strange creamy half-figure making straight for the ruins. He followed it as well as he could; as before, he was impeded by the ivy and weeds, and the figure awaited him; as before, it made straight for the heap of masonry and disappeared as soon as Mr. Batchel was at liberty to follow.

There were no dungeons, or subterranean premises beneath the manor house. It had never been more than a house of residence, and the building had been purely domestic in character. Mr. Batchel was convinced that his adventure would prove unromantic, and felt some impatience at losing again, what he had begun to call his triangular friend. If this friend wanted anything, it was not easy to say why he had so tamely disappeared. There seemed nothing to be done but to wait until he came out again.

Mr. Batchel had a pipe in his pocket, and he seated himself upon the base of a sundial within full view of the spot. He filled and smoked his pipe, sitting in momentary expectation of some further sign, but nothing appeared. He heard the hedgehogs moving about him in the undergrowth, and now and then the sound of a restless bird overhead, otherwise all was still. He smoked a second pipe without any further discovery, and that finished, he knocked out the ashes against his boot, walked to the mound, near to which his labelled stick was lying, thrust the stick into the place where the figure had disappeared, and went back to bed, where he was rewarded with five hours of sound sleep.

Mr. Batchel had made up his mind that the next day ought to be a day of disclosure. He was early at the manor house, this time provided with the gardener's pick, and a spade. He thrust the pick into the place from which he had removed his mark, and loosened the rubbish thoroughly. With his hands, and with his spade, he was not long in reducing the size of the heap by about one-half, and there he found more coins.

There were three more crowns, two half-crowns, and a dozen or so of smaller coins. All these Mr. Batchel wrapped carefully in his handkerchief, and after a few minutes rest went on with his task. As it proved, the task was nearly over. Some strips of oak about nine inches long, were next uncovered, and then, what Mr. Batchel had begun to expect, the lid of a box, with the hinges still attached. It lay, face downwards, upon a flat stone. It proved, when he had taken it up, to be almost unsoiled, and above a long and wide slit in the lid was the gilded legend, "for ye poore" in the graceful lettering and the redundant spelling of two centuries ago.

The meaning of all this Mr. Batchel was not long in interpreting. That the box and its contents had fallen and been broken amongst the masonry, was evident enough. It was as evident that it had been concealed in one of the walls brought down by the fire, and Mr. Batchel had no doubt at all that he had been in the company of a thief, who had once stolen the poor-box from the church. His task seemed to be at an end, a further rummage revealed nothing new. Mr. Batchel carefully collected the fragments of the box, and left the place.

His next act cannot be defended. He must have been aware that these coins were "treasure trove," and therefore the property of the Crown. In spite of this, he determined to convert them into current coin, as he well knew how, and to apply the proceeds to the Inundation Fund about which he was so anxious. Treating them as his own property, he cleaned them all, as he had cleaned the two crowns, sent them to an antiquarian friend in London to sell for him, and awaited the result. The lid of the poor box he still preserves as a relic of the adventure.

His antiquarian friend did not keep him long waiting. The coins had been eagerly bought, and the price surpassed any expectation that Mr. Batchel had allowed himself to entertain. He had sent the package to London on Saturday morning. Upon the following Tuesday, the last post in the evening brought a cheque for twenty guineas. The brief subscription list of the Inundation Fund lay upon his desk, and he at once entered the amount he had so strangely come by, but could not immediately decide upon its description. Leaving the line blank, therefore, he merely wrote down £21 in the cash column, to be assigned to its source in some suitable form of words when he should have found time to frame them.

In this state he left the subscription list upon his desk, when he retired for the night. It occurred to him as he was undressing, that the twenty guineas might suitably be described as a "restitution," and so he determined to enter it upon the line he had left vacant. As he reconsidered the matter in the morning, he saw no reason to alter his decision, and he went straight from his bedroom to his desk to make the entry and have done with it.

There was an incident in the adventure, however, upon which Mr. Batchel had not reckoned. As he approached the list, he saw, to his amazement, that the line had been filled in. In a crabbed, elongated hand was written, "At last, St. Matt. v. 26."

What may seem more strange is that the handwriting was familiar to Mr. Batchel, he could not at first say why. His memory, however, in such matters, was singularly good, and before breakfast was over he felt sure of having identified the writer.

His confidence was not misplaced. He went to the parish chest, whose contents he had thoroughly examined in past intervals of leisure, and took out the roll of parish constable's accounts. In a few minutes he discovered the handwriting of which he was in search. It was unmistakably that of Salathiel Thrapston, constable from 1705—1710, who met his death in the latter year, whilst in the execution of his duty. The reader will scarcely need to be reminded of the text of the Gospel at the place of reference—

Thou shalt by no means come out thence till thou hast paid the uttermost farthing.

Lubrietta

For the better understanding of this narrative we shall furnish the reader with a few words of introduction. It amounts to no more than a brief statement of facts which Mr. Batchel obtained from the lady principal of the European college in Puna, but the facts nevertheless are important. The narrative itself was obtained from Mr. Batchel with difficulty: he was disposed to regard it as unsuitable for publication because of the delicate nature of the situations with which it deals. When, however, it was made clear to him that it would be recorded in such a manner as would interest only a very select body of readers, his scruples were overcome, and he was induced to communicate the experience now to be related. Those who read it will not fail to see that they are in a manner pledged to deal very discreetly with the knowledge they are privileged to share.

Lubrietta Rodria is described by her lady principal as an attractive and high-spirited girl of seventeen, belonging to the Purple of Indian commerce. Her nationality was not precisely known; but drawing near, as she did, to a marriageable age, and being courted by more than one eligible suitor, she was naturally an object of great interest to her schoolfellows, with whom her personal beauty and amiable temper had always made her a favourite. She was not, the lady principal thought, a girl who would be regarded in Christian countries as of very high principle; but none the less, she was one whom it was impossible not to like.

Her career at the college had ended sensationally. She had

been immoderately anxious about her final examination, and its termination had found her in a state of collapse. They had at once removed her to her father's house in the country, where she received such nursing and assiduous attention as her case required. It was apparently of no avail. For three weeks she lay motionless, deprived of speech, and voluntarily, taking no food. Then for a further period of ten days she lay in a plight still more distressing. She lost all consciousness, and, despite the assurance of the doctors, her parents could hardly be persuaded that she lived.

Her *fiancé* who by this time had been declared, was in despair, not only from natural affection for Lubrietta, but from remorse. It was his intellectual ambition that had incited her to the eagerness in study which was threatening such dire results, and it was well understood that neither of the lovers would survive these anxious days of watching if they were not to be survived by both.

After ten days, however, a change supervened. Lubrietta came back to life amid the frenzied rejoicing of the household and all her circle. She recovered her health and strength with incredible speed, and within three months was married—as the lady principal had cause to believe, with the happiest prospects.

★ ★ ★ ★ ★ ★ ★ ★ ★ ★

Mr. Batchel had not, whilst residing at Stoneground, lost touch with the university which had given him his degree, and in which he had formerly held one or two minor offices. He had earned no great distinction as a scholar, but had taken a degree in honours, and was possessed of a useful amount of general knowledge, and in this he found not only constant pleasure, but also occasional profit.

The university had made herself, for better or worse, an examiner of a hundred times as many students as she could teach; her system of examinations had extended to the very limits of the British Empire, and her certificates of proficiency were coveted in every quarter of the globe.

In the examination of these students, Mr. Batchel, who had considerable experience in teaching, was annually employed. Papers from all parts of the world were to be found littered about his study, and the examination of these papers called for some weeks of strenuous labour at every year's end. As the weeks passed, he would anxiously watch the growth of a neat stack of papers in the corner of the room, which indicated the number to which marks had been assigned and reported to Cambridge. The day upon which the last of these was laid in its place was a day of satisfaction, second only to that which later on brought him a substantial cheque to remunerate him for his labours.

During this period of special effort, Mr. Batchel's servants had their share of its discomforts. The chairs and tables they wanted to dust and to arrange, were loaded with papers which they were forbidden to touch; and although they were warned against showing visitors into any room where these papers were lying, Mr. Batchel would inconsiderately lay them in every room he had. The privacy of his study, however, where the work was chiefly done, was strictly guarded, and no one was admitted there unless by Mr. Batchel himself.

Imagine his annoyance, therefore, when he returned from an evening engagement at the beginning of the month of January, and found a stranger seated in the study! Yet the annoyance was not long in subsiding. The visitor was a lady, and as she sat by the lamp, a glance was enough to shew that she was young, and very beautiful. The interest which this young lady excited in Mr. Batchel was altogether unusual, as unusual as was the visit of such a person at such a time. His conjecture was that she had called to give him notice of a marriage, but he was really charmed by her presence, and was quite content to find her in no haste to state her errand. The manner, however, of the lady was singular, for neither by word nor movement did she show that she was conscious of Mr. Batchel's entry into the room.

He began at length with his customary formula "What can I have the pleasure of doing for you?" and when, at the sound of his voice, she turned her fine dark eyes upon him, he saw that they were wet with tears.

Mr. Batchel was now really moved. As a tear fell upon the lady's cheek, she raised her hand as if to conceal it—a brilliant sapphire sparkling in the lamplight as she did so. And then the lady's distress, and the exquisite grace of her presence, altogether overcame him. There stole upon him a strange feeling of tenderness which he supposed to be paternal, but knew nevertheless to be indiscreet. He was a prudent man, with strict notions of propriety, so that, ostensibly with a view to giving the lady a few minutes in which to recover her composure, he quietly left the study and went into another room, to pull himself together.

Mr. Batchel, like most solitary men, had a habit of talking to himself. "It is of no use, R. B.," he said, "to pretend that you have retired on this damsel's account. If you don't take care, you'll make a fool of yourself." He took up from the table a volume of the *encyclopaedia* in which, the day before, he had been looking up Pestalozzi, and turned over the pages in search of something to restore his equanimity. An article on perspective proved to be the very thing. Wholly unromantic in character, its copious presentment of hard fact relieved his mind, and he was soon threading his way along paths of knowledge to which he was little accustomed.

He applied his remedy with such persistence that when four or five minutes had passed, he felt sufficiently composed to return to the study. He framed, as he went, a suitable form of words with which to open the conversation, and took with him his register of Banns of Marriage, of which he thought he foresaw the need. As he opened the study-door, the book fell from his hands to the ground, so completely was he overcome by surprise, for he found the room empty. The lady had disappeared; her chair stood vacant before him.

Mr. Batchel sat down for a moment, and then rang the bell. It was answered by the boy who always attended upon him.

"When did the lady go?" asked Mr. Batchel.

The boy looked bewildered.

"The lady you showed into the study before I came."

"Please, sir, I never shown anyone into the study; I never do when you're out."

"There was a lady here," said Mr. Batchel, "when I returned."

The boy now looked incredulous.

"Did you not let someone out just now?"

"No, sir," said the boy. "I put the chain on the front door as soon as you came in."

This was conclusive. The chain upon the hall-door was an ancient and cumbrous thing, and could not be manipulated without considerable effort, and a great deal of noise. Mr. Batchel released the boy, and began to think furiously. He was not, as the reader is well aware, without some experience of the supernormal side of nature, and he knew of course that the visit of this enthralling lady had a purpose. He was beginning to know, however, that it had had an effect. He sat before his fire reproducing her image, and soon gave it up in disgust because his imagination refused to do her justice. He could recover the details of her appearance, but could combine them into nothing that would reproduce the impression she had first made upon him.

He was unable now to concentrate his attention upon the examination papers lying on his table. His mind wandered so often to the other topic that he felt himself to be in danger of marking the answers unfairly. He turned away from his work, therefore, and moved to another chair, where he sat down to read. It was the chair in which she herself had sat, and he made no attempt to pretend that he had chosen it on any other account. He had, in fact, made some discoveries about himself during the last half-hour, and he gave himself another surprise when he came to select his book.

In the ordinary course of what he had supposed to be his nature, he would certainly have returned to the article on perspective; it was lying open in the next room, and he had read no more than a tenth part of it. But instead of that, his thoughts went back to a volume he had but once opened, and that for no more than two minutes. He had received the book, by way of birthday present, early in the preceding year, from a relative who had bestowed either no consideration at all, or else a great deal of cunning, upon its selection. It was a collection of 17th century lyrics, which Mr. Batchel's single glance had sufficed to condemn. Regarding the one lyric he had read as a sort of literary freak, he had banished the book to one of the spare bedrooms, and had never seen it since. And now, after this long interval, the absurd lines which his eye had but once lighted upon, were recurring to his mind:

Fair, sweet, and young, receive a prize
Reserved for your victorious eyes;

and so far from thinking them absurd, as he now recalled them, he went upstairs to fetch the book, in which he was soon absorbed. The lyrics no longer seemed unreasonable. He felt conscious, as he read one after another, of a side of nature that he had strangely neglected, and was obliged to admit that the men whose feelings were set forth in the various sonnets and poems had a fine gift of expression.

Thus, whilst I look for her in vain,
Methinks I am a child again.
And of my shadow am a-chasing.
For all her graces are to me
Like apparitions that I see,
But never can come near th' embracing.

No! these men were not, as he had formerly supposed, writing with air, and he felt ashamed at having used the term "freak" at their expense.

Mr. Batchel read more of the lyrics, some of them twice, and one of them much oftener. That one he began to commit to memory, and since the household had retired to rest, to recite aloud. He had been unaware that literature contained anything so beautiful, and as he looked again at the book to recover an expression his memory had lost, a tear fell upon the page. It was a thing so extraordinary that Mr. Batchel first looked at the ceiling, but when he found that it was indeed a tear from his own eye he was immoderately pleased with himself. Had not she also shed a tear as she sat upon the same chair? The fact seemed to draw them together.

Contemplation of this sort was, however, a luxury to be enjoyed in something like moderation. Mr. Batchel soon laid down his lyric and savagely began to add up columns of marks, by way of discipline; and when he had totalled several pages of these, respect for his normal self had returned with sufficient force to take him off to bed.

The matter of his dreams, or whether he dreamed at all, has not been disclosed. He awoke, at any rate, in a calmer state of mind, and such romantic thoughts as remained were effectually dispelled by the sight of his own countenance when he began to shave. "Fancy you spouting lyrics," he said, as he dabbed the brush upon his mouth, and by the time he was ready for breakfast he pronounced himself cured.

The prosaic labours awaiting him in the study were soon forced upon his notice, and for once he did not regret it. Amongst the letters lying upon the breakfast table was one from the secretary who controlled the system of examination. The form of the envelope was too familiar to leave him in doubt as to what it contained. It was a letter which, to a careful man like Mr. Batchel, seemed to have the nature of a reproof, inasmuch as it probably asked for information which it had already been his duty to furnish.

The contents of the envelope, when he had impatiently torn it open, answered to his expectation—he was formally requested to supply the name and the marks of candidate No. 1004, and he wondered, as he ate his breakfast, how he had omitted to return them. He hunted out the paper of No. 1004 as soon as the meal was over. The candidate proved to be one Lubrietta Rodria, of whom, of course, he had never heard, and her answers had all been marked. He could not understand why they should have been made the subject of enquiry.

He took her papers in his hand, and looked at them again

as he stood with his back to the fire, having lit the pipe which invariably followed his breakfast, and then he discovered something much harder to understand. The marks were not his own. In place of the usual sketchy numerals, hardly decipherable to any but himself, he saw figures which were carefully formed; and the marks assigned to the first answer, as he saw it on the uppermost sheet, were higher than the maximum number obtainable for that question.

Mr. Batchel laid down his pipe and seated himself at the table. He was greatly puzzled. As he turned over the sheets of No. 1004 he found all the other questions marked in like manner, and making a total of half as much again as the highest possible number. "Who the dickens," he said, using a meaningless, but not uncommon expression, "has been playing with this; and how came I to pass it over?" The need of the moment, however, was to furnish the proper marks to the secretary at Cambridge, and Mr. Batchel proceeded to read No. 1004 right through.

He soon found that he had read it all before, and the matter began to bristle with queries. It proved, in fact, to be a paper over which he had spent some time, and for a singularly interesting reason. He had learned from a friend in the Indian Civil Service that an exaggerated value was often placed by ambitious Indians and Cingalese upon a European education, and that many aspiring young men declined to take a wife who had not passed this very examination. It was to Mr. Batchel a disquieting reflection that his blue pencil was not only marking mistakes, but might at the same time be cancelling matrimonial engagements, and his friend's communication had made him scrupulously careful in examining the work of young ladies in Oriental schools.

The matter had occurred to him at once as he had examined the answers of Lubrietta Rodria. He perfectly remembered the question upon which her success depended. A problem in logic had been answered by a rambling and worthless argument, to which, somehow, the right conclusion was appended: the conclusion might be a happy guess, or it might have been secured by less honest means, but Mr. Batchel, following his usual practice, gave no marks for it.

It was not here that he found any cause for hesitation, but when he came to the end of the paper and found that the candidate had only just failed, he had turned back to the critical question, imagined an eligible bachelor awaiting the result of the examination, and then, after a period of vacillation, had hastily put the symbol of failure upon the paper lest he should be tempted to bring his own charity to the rescue of the candidate's logic, and unfairly add the three marks which would suffice to pass her.

As he now read the answer for the second time, the same pitiful thought troubled him, and this time more than before; for over the edge of the paper of No. 1004 there persistently arose the image of the young lady with the sapphire ring. It directed the current of his thoughts. Suppose that Lubrietta Rodria were anything like that! and what if the arguments of No. 1004 were worthless! Young ladies were notoriously weak in argument, and as strong in conclusions! and after all, the conclusion was correct, and ought not a correct conclusion to have its marks? There followed much more to the same purpose, and in the end Mr. Batchel stultified himself by adding the necessary three marks, and passing the candidate.

"This comes precious near to being a job," he remarked, as he entered the marks upon the form and sealed it in the envelope, "but No. 1004 must pass, this time." He enclosed in the envelope a request to know why the marks had been asked for, since they had certainly been returned in their proper place. A brief official reply informed him next day that the marks he had returned exceeded the maximum, and must, therefore, have been wrongly entered.

"This," said Mr. Batchel, "is a curious coincidence."

Curious as it certainly was, it was less curious than what immediately followed. It was Mr. Batchel's practice to avoid any delay in returning these official papers, and he went out, there and then, to post his envelope. The post office was no more than a hundred yards from his door, and in three minutes he was in his study again. The first object that met his eye there was a beautiful sapphire ring lying upon the papers of No. 1004, which had remained upon the table.

Mr. Batchel at once recognised the ring. "I knew it was precious near a job," he said, "but I didn't know that it was as near as this."

He took up the ring and examined it. It looked like a ring of great value; the stone was large and brilliant, and the setting was of fine workmanship. "Now what on earth," said Mr. Batchel, "am I to do with this?"

The nearest jeweller to Stoneground was a competent and experienced tradesman of the old school. He was a member of the local Natural History Society, and in that capacity Mr. Batchel had made intimate acquaintance with him. To this jeweller, therefore, he carried the ring, and asked him what he thought of it.

"I'll give you forty pounds for it," said the jeweller.

Mr. Batchel replied that the ring was not his. "What about the make of it?" he asked. "Is it English?"

The jeweller replied that it was unmistakably Indian.

"You are sure?" said Mr. Batchel.

"Certain," said the jeweller. "Major Ackroyd brought home one like it, all but the stone, from Puna; I repaired it for him last year."

The information was enough, if not more than enough, for Mr. Batchel. He begged a suitable case from his friend the jeweller, and within an hour had posted the ring to Miss Lubrietta Rodria at the European college in Puna. At the same time he wrote to the principal the letter whose answer is embodied in the preface to this narrative.

Having done this, Mr. Batchel felt more at ease. He had given Lubrietta Rodria what he amiably called the benefit of the doubt, but it should never be said that he had been bribed.

The rest of his papers he marked with fierce justice. A great deal of the work, in his zeal, he did twice over, but his conscience amply requited him for the superfluous labour. The last paper was marked within a day of the allotted time, Mr. Batchel shortly afterwards received his cheque, and was glad to think that the whole matter was at an end.

★ ★ ★ ★ ★ ★ ★ ★ ★ ★

That Lubrietta had been absent from India whilst her relatives and attendants were trying to restore her to consciousness, he had good reason to know. His friends, for the most part, took a very narrow view of human nature and its possibilities, so that he kept his experience, for a long time, to himself; there were personal reasons for not discussing the incident. The reader has been already told upon what understanding it is recorded here.

There remains, however, an episode which Mr. Batchel all but managed to suppress. Upon the one occasion when he allowed himself to speak of this matter, he was being pressed for a description of the sapphire ring, and was not very successful in his attempt to describe it. There was no reason, of course, why this should lay his good faith under suspicion. Few of us could pass an examination upon objects with which we are supposed to be familiar, or say which of our tables have three legs, and which four.

One of Mr. Batchel's auditors, however, took a captious view of the matter, and brusquely remarked, in imitation of a more famous sceptic, "I don't believe there's no sich a thing."

Mr. Batchel, of course, recognised the phrase, and it was his eagerness to establish his credit that committed him at this point to a last disclosure about Lubrietta. He drew a sapphire ring from his pocket, handed it to the incredulous auditor, and addressed him in the manner of Mrs. Gamp.

"What! you bage creetur, have I had this ring three year or more to be told there ain't no sech a thing. Go along with you."

"But I thought the ring was sent back," said more than one.

"How did you come by it?" said all the others.

Mr. Batchel thereupon admitted that he had closed his story prematurely. About six weeks after the return of the ring to Puna

70

he had found it once again upon his table, returned through the post. Enclosed in the package was a note which Mr. Batchel, being now committed to this part of the story, also passed round for inspection It ran as follows:—

Accept the ring, dear one, and wear it for my sake. Fail not to think sometimes of her whom you have made happy.—L. R.

"What on earth am I to do with this?" Mr. Batchel had asked himself again. And this time he had answered the question, after the briefest possible delay, by slipping the ring upon his fourth finger.

The book of Lyrics remained downstairs amongst the books in constant use. Mr. Batchel can repeat at least half of the collection from memory.

He knows well enough that such terms as "dear one" are addressed to bald gentlemen only in a Pickwickian sense, but even with that sense the letter gives him pleasure.

He admits that he thinks very often of "her whom he has made happy," but that he cannot exclude from his thoughts at these times an ungenerous regret. It is that he has also made happy a nameless Oriental gentleman whom he presumptuously calls "the other fellow."

The Rockery

The vicar's garden at Stoneground has certainly been enclosed for more than seven centuries, and during the whole of that time its almost sacred privacy has been regarded as permanent and unchangeable. It has remained for the innovators of later and more audacious days to hint that it might be given into other hands, and still carry with it no curse that should make a new possessor hasten to undo his irreverence. Whether there can be warrant for such confidence, time will show. The experiences already related will show that the privacy of the garden has been counted upon both by good men and worse. And here is a story, in its way, more strange than any.

By way of beginning, it may be well to describe a part of the garden not hitherto brought into notice. That part lies on the western boundary, where the garden slopes down to a sluggish stream, hardly a stream at all, locally known as the Lode. The Lode bounds the garden on the west along its whole length, and there the moorhen builds her nest, and the kingfisher is sometimes, but in these days too rarely, seen. But the centre of vision, as it were, of this western edge lies in a cluster of tall elms. Towards these all the garden paths converge, and about their base is raised a bank of earth, upon which is heaped a rockery of large stones lately overgrown with ferns.

Mr. Batchel's somewhat prim taste in gardening had long resented this disorderly bank. In more than one place in his garden had wild confusion given place to a park-like trimness, and there were not a few who would say that the change was not for the better. Mr. Batchel, however, went his own way, and in due time determined to remove the rockery. He was puzzled by its presence; he could see no reason why a bank should have been raised about the feet of the elms, and surmounted with stones; not a ray of sunshine ever found its way there, and none but coarse and uninteresting plants had established themselves. Whoever had raised the bank had done it ignorantly, or with some purpose not easy for Mr. Batchel to conjecture.

Upon a certain day, therefore, in the early part of December, when the garden had been made comfortable for its winter rest, he began, with the assistance of his gardener, to remove the stones into another place.

We do but speak according to custom in this matter, and there are few readers who will not suspect the truth, which is that the gardener began to remove the stones, whilst Mr. Batchel stood by and delivered criticisms of very slight value. Such strength, in fact, as Mr. Batchel possessed had concentrated itself upon the mind, and somewhat neglected his body, and what he called help, during his presence in the garden, was called by another name when the gardener and his boy were left to themselves, with full freedom of speech.

There were few of the stones rolled down by the gardener that Mr. Batchel could even have moved, but his astonishment at their size soon gave place to excitement at their appearance. His antiquarian tastes were strong, and were soon busily engaged. For, as the stones rolled down, his eyes were feasted, in a rapid succession, by capitals of columns, fragments of moulded arches and mullions, and other relics of ecclesiastical building.

Repeatedly did he call the gardener down from his work to put these fragments together, and before long there were several complete lengths of arcading laid upon the path. Stones which, perhaps, had been separated for centuries, once more came together, and Mr. Batchel, rubbing his hands in excited satisfaction, declared that he might recover the best parts of a church by the time the rockery had been demolished.

The interest of the gardener in such matters was of a milder kind. "We must go careful," he merely observed, "when we come to the organ." They went on removing more and more stones, until at length the whole bank was laid bare, and Mr. Batchel's chief purpose achieved. How the stones were carefully arranged, and set up in other parts of the garden, is well known, and need not concern us now.

One detail, however, must not be omitted. A large and stout stake of yew, evidently of considerable age, but nevertheless quite sound, stood exposed after the clearing of the bank. There was no obvious reason for its presence, but it had been well driven in, so well that the strength of the gardener, or, if it made any difference, of the gardener and Mr. Batchel together, failed even to shake it. It was not unsightly, and might have remained where it was, had not the gardener exclaimed, "This is the very thing we want for the pump." It was so obviously "the very thing" that its removal was then and there decided upon.

The pump referred to was a small iron pump used to draw water from the lode. It had been affixed to many posts in turn, and defied them all to hold it. Not that the pump was at fault. It was a trifling affair enough. But the pumpers were usually garden-boys, whose impatient energy had never failed, before many days, to wriggle the pump away from its supports. When the gardener had, upon one occasion, spent half a day in attaching it firmly to a post, they had at once shaken out the post itself. Since, therefore, the matter was causing daily inconvenience, and the gardener becoming daily more concerned for his reputation as a rough carpenter, it was natural for him to exclaim, "This is the very thing." It was a better stake than he had ever used, and as had just been made evident, a stake that the ground would hold.

"Yes!" said Mr. Batchel, "it is the very thing; but can we get it up?" The gardener always accepted this kind of query as a challenge, and replied only by taking up a pick and setting to work, Mr. Batchel, as usual, looking on, and making, every now and then, a fruitless suggestion. After a few minutes, however, he made somewhat more than a suggestion. He darted forward and laid his hand upon the pick. "Don't you see some copper?" he asked quickly.

Every man who digs knows what a hiding place there is in the earth. The monotony of spade work is always relieved by a hope of turning up something unexpected. Treasure lies dimly behind all these hopes, so that the gardener, having seen Mr. Batchel excited over so much that was precious from his own point of view, was quite ready to look for something of value to an ordinary reasonable man. Copper might lead to silver, and that, in turn, to gold. At Mr. Batchel's eager question, therefore, he peered into the hole he had made, and examined everything there that might suggest the rounded form of a coin.

He soon saw what had arrested Mr. Batchel. There was a lustrous scratch on the side of the stake, evidently made by the pick, and though the metal was copper, plainly enough, the gardener felt that he had been deceived, and would have gone on with his work. Copper of that sort gave him no sort of excitement, and only a feeble interest.

Mr. Batchel, however, was on his hands and knees. There was a small irregular plate of copper nailed to the stake; without any difficulty he tore it away from the nails, and soon scraped it clean with a shaving of wood; then, rising to his feet, he examined his find.

There was an inscription upon it, so legible as to need no deciphering. It had been roughly and effectually made with a hammer and nail, the letters being formed by series of holes punched deeply into the metal, and what he read was:—

MOVE NOT THIS STAKE, NOV. 1, 1702.

But to move the stake was what Mr. Batchel had determined upon, and the metal plate he held in his hand interested him chiefly as showing how long the post had been there. He had happened, as he supposed, upon an ancient landmark. The discovery, recorded elsewhere, of a well, near to the edge of his present lawn, had shown him that his premises had once been differently arranged. One of the minor antiquarian tasks he had set himself was to discover and record the old arrangement, and he felt that the position of this stake would help him. He felt no doubt of its being a point upon the western limit of the garden; not improbably marked in this way to show where the garden began, and where ended the ancient hauling-way, which had been secured to the public for purposes of navigation.

The gardener, meanwhile, was proceeding with his work. With no small difficulty he removed the rubble and clay which accounted for the firmness of the stake. It grew dark as the work went on, and a distant clock struck five before it was completed. Five was the hour at which the gardener usually went home; his day began early. He was not, however, a man to leave a small job unfinished, and he went on loosening the earth with his pick, and trying the effect, at intervals, upon the firmness of the stake.

It naturally began to give, and could be moved from side to side through a space of some few inches. He lifted out the loosened stones, and loosened more. His pick struck iron, which, after loosening, proved to be links of a rusted chain. "They've buried a lot of rubbish in this hole," he remarked, as he went on loosening the chain, which, in the growing darkness, could hardly be seen. Mr. Batchel, meanwhile, occupied himself in a simpler task of working the stake to and fro, by way of loosening its hold. Ultimately it began to move with greater freedom. The gardener laid down his tool and grasped the stake, which his master was still holding; their combined efforts succeeded at once; the stake was lifted out.

It turned out to be furnished with an unusually long and sharp point, which explained the firmness of its hold upon the ground. The gardener carried it to the neighbourhood of the pump, in readiness for its next purpose, and made ready to go home. He would drive the stake tomorrow, he said, in the new place, and make the pump so secure that not even the boys could shake it. He also spoke of some designs he had upon the chain, should it prove to be of any considerable length. He was an ingenious man, and his skill in converting discarded articles to new uses was embarrassing to his master.

Mr. Batchel, as has been said, was a prim gardener, and he had no liking for makeshift devices. He had that day seen his runner beans trained upon a length of old gas-piping, and had no intention of leaving the gardener in possession of such a treasure as a rusty chain. What he said, however, and said with truth, was that he wanted the chain for himself. He had no practical use for it, and hardly expected it to yield him any interest. But a chain buried in 1702 must be examined—nothing ancient comes amiss to a man of antiquarian tastes.

Mr. Batchel had noticed, whilst the gardener had been carrying away the stake, that the chain lay very loosely in the earth. The pick had worked well round it. He said, therefore, that the chain must be lifted out and brought to him upon the morrow, bade his gardener good night, and went in to his fireside.

This will appear to the reader to be a record of the merest trifles, but all readers will accept the reminder that there is no such thing as a trifle, and that what appears to be trivial has that appearance only so long as it stands alone.

Regarded in the light of their consequences, those matters which have seemed to be least in importance, turn out, often enough, to be the greatest. And these trifling occupations, as we may call them for the last time, of Mr. Batchel and the gardener, had consequences which shall now be set down as Mr. Batchel himself narrated them. But we must take events in their order. At present Mr. Batchel is at his fireside, and his gardener at home with his family. The stake is removed, and the hole, in which lies some sort of an iron chain, is exposed.

Upon this particular evening Mr. Batchel was dining out. He was a good natured man, with certain mild powers of entertainment, and his presence as an occasional guest was not unacceptable at some of the more considerable houses of the neighbourhood. And let us hasten to observe that he was not a guest who made any great impression upon the larders or the cellars of his hosts. He liked port, but he liked it only of good quality, and in small quantity.

When he returned from a dinner party, therefore, he was never either in a surfeited condition of body, or in any confusion of mind. Not uncommonly after his return upon such occasions did he perform accurate work. Unfinished contributions to sundry local journals were seldom absent from his desk. They were his means of recreation. There they awaited convenient intervals of leisure, and Mr. Batchel was accustomed to say that of these intervals he found none so productive as a late hour, or hour and a half, after a dinner party.

Upon the evening in question he returned, about an hour before midnight, from dining at the house of a retired officer residing in the neighbourhood, and the evening had been somewhat less enjoyable than usual. He had taken in to dinner a young lady who had too persistently assailed him with antiquarian questions. Now Mr. Batchel did not like talking what he regarded as "shop," and was not much at home with young ladies, to whom he knew that, in the nature of things, he could be but imperfectly acceptable. With infinite good will towards them, and a genuine liking for their presence, he felt that he had but little to offer them in exchange. There was so little in common between his life and theirs. He felt distinctly at his worst when he found himself treated as a mere scrapbook of information. It made him seem, as he would express it, dehumanised.

Upon this particular evening the young lady allotted to him, perhaps at her own request, had made a scrapbook of him, and he had returned home somewhat discontented, if also somewhat amused. His discontent arose from having been deprived of the general conversation he so greatly, but so rarely, enjoyed. His amusement was caused by the incongruity between a very light-hearted young lady and the subject upon which she had made him talk, for she had talked of nothing else but modes of burial.

He began to recall the conversation as he lit his pipe and dropped into his armchair. She had either been reflecting deeply upon the matter, or, as seemed to Mr. Batchel, more probable, had read something and half forgotten it. He recalled her questions, and the answers by which he had vainly tried to lead her to a more attractive topic. For example:

She: Will you tell me why people were buried at cross roads?

He: Well, consecrated ground was so, jealously guarded that a criminal would be held to have forfeited the right to be buried amongst Christian folk. His friends would therefore choose cross roads where there was set a wayside cross, and make his grave at the foot of it. In some of my journeys in Scotland I have seen crosses.

But the young lady had refused to be led into Scotland. She had stuck to her subject.

She: Why have coffins come back into use? There is nothing in our Burial Service about a coffin.

He: True, and the use of the coffin is due, in part, to an ignorant notion of confining the corpse, lest, like Hamlet's father, he should walk the earth. You will have noticed that the corpse is always carried out of the house feet foremost, to suggest a final exit, and that the grave is often covered with a heavy slab. Very curious epitaphs are to be found on these slabs.

But she was not to be drawn into the subject of epitaphs. She had made him tell of other devices for confining spirits to their prison, and securing the peace of the living, especially of those adopted in the case of violent and mischievous men. Altogether an unusual sort of young lady.

The conversation, however, had revived his memories of what was, after all, a matter of some interest, and he determined to look through his parish registers for records of exceptional burials. He was surprised at himself for never having done it. He dismissed the matter from his mind for the time being, and as it was a bright moonlight night he thought he would finish his pipe in the garden.

Therefore, although midnight was close at hand, he strolled complacently round his garden, enjoying the light of the moon no less than in the daytime he would have enjoyed the sun; and thus it was that he arrived at the scene of his labours upon the old rockery. There was more light than there had been at the end of the afternoon, and when he had walked up the bank, and stood over the hole we have already described, he could distinctly see the few exposed links of the iron chain. Should he remove it at once to a place of safety, out of the way of the gardener? It was about time for bed. The city clocks were then striking midnight. He would let the chain decide. If it came out easily he would remove it; otherwise, it should remain until morning.

The chain came out more than easily. It seemed to have a force within itself. He gave but a slight tug at the free end with a view of ascertaining what resistance he had to encounter, and immediately found himself lying upon his back with the chain in his hand. His back had fortunately turned towards an elm three feet away which broke his fall, but there had been violence enough to cause him no little surprise.

The effort he had made was so slight that he could not account for having lost his feet; and being a careful man, he was a little anxious about his evening coat, which he was still wearing. The chain, however, was in his hand, and he made haste to coil it into a portable shape, and to return to the house.

Some fifty yards from the spot was the northern boundary of the garden, a long wall with a narrow lane beyond. It was not unusual, even at this hour of the night, to hear footsteps there. The lane was used by railway men, who passed to and from their work at all hours, as also by some who returned late from entertainments in the neighbouring city.

But Mr. Batchel, as he turned back to the house, with his chain over one arm, heard more than footsteps. He heard for a few moments the unmistakable sound of a scuffle, and then a piercing cry, loud and sharp, and a noise of running. It was such a cry as could only have come from one in urgent need of help.

Mr. Batchel dropped his chain. The garden wall was some ten feet high and he had no means of scaling it. But he ran quickly into the house, passed out by the hall door into the street, and so towards the lane without a moment's loss of time.

Before he has gone many yards he sees a man running from

the lane with his clothing in great disorder, and this man, at the sight of Mr. Batchel, darts across the road, runs along in the shadow of an opposite wall and attempts to escape.

The man is known well enough to Mr. Batchel. It is one Stephen Medd, a respectable and sensible man, by occupation a shunter, and Mr. Batchel at once calls out to ask what has happened. Stephen, however, makes no reply but continues to run along the shadow of the wall, whereupon Mr. Batchel crosses over and intercepts him, and again asks what is amiss. Stephen answers wildly and breathlessly, "I'm not going to stop here, let me go home."

As Mr. Batchel lays his hand upon the man's arm and draws him into the light of the moon, it is seen that his face is streaming with blood from a wound near the eye.

He is somewhat calmed by the familiar voice of Mr. Batchel, and is about to speak, when another scream is heard from the lane. The voice is that of a boy or woman, and no sooner does Stephen hear it than he frees himself violently from Mr. Batchel and makes away towards his home. With no less speed does Mr. Batchel make for the lane, and finds about half way down a boy lying on the ground wounded and terrified.

At first the boy clings to the ground, but he, too, is soon reassured by Mr. Batchel's voice, and allows himself to be lifted on to his feet. His wound is also in the face, and Mr. Batchel takes the boy into his house, bathes and plasters his wound, and soon restores him to something like calm. He is what is termed a call-boy, employed by the Railway Company to awaken drivers at all hours, and give them their instructions.

Mr. Batchel is naturally impatient for the moment he can question the boy about his assailant, who is presumably also the assailant of Stephen Medd. No one had been visible in the lane, though the moon shone upon it from end to end. At the first available moment, therefore, he asks the boy, "Who did this?"

The answer came, without any hesitation, "Nobody."

"There was nobody there," he said, "and all of a sudden somebody hit me with an iron thing."

Then Mr. Batchel asked, "Did you see Stephen Medd?" He was becoming greatly puzzled.

The boy replied that he had seen Mr. Medd "a good bit in front," with nobody near him, and that all of a sudden someone knocked him down.

Further questioning seemed useless. Mr. Batchel saw the boy to his home, left him at the door, and returned to bed, but not to sleep. He could not cease from thinking, and he could think of nothing but assaults from invisible hands. Morning seemed long in coming, but came at last.

Mr. Batchel was up betimes and made a very poor breakfast. Dallying with the morning paper, rather than reading it, his eye was arrested by a headline about "Mysterious assaults in Elmham." He felt that he had mysteries of his own to occupy him and was in no mood to be interested in more assaults. But he had some knowledge of Elmham, a small town ten miles distant from Stoneground, and he read the brief paragraph, which contained no more than the substance of a telegram.

It said, however, that three persons had been victims of unaccountable assaults. Two of them had escaped with slight injuries, but the third, a young woman, was dangerously wounded, though still alive and conscious. She declared that she was quite alone in her house and had been suddenly struck with great violence by what felt like a piece of iron, and that she must have bled to death but for a neighbour who heard her cries. The neighbour had at once looked out and seen nobody, but had bravely gone to her friend's assistance.

Mr. Batchel laid down his newspaper considerably impressed, as was natural, by the resemblance of these tragedies to what he had witnessed himself. He was in no condition, after his excitement and his sleepless night, to do his usual work. His mind reverted to the conversation at the dinner party and the trifle of antiquarian research it had suggested. Such occupation had often served him when he found himself suffering from a cold, or otherwise indisposed for more serious work. He would get the registers and collect what entries there might be of irregular burial. He found only one such entry, but that one was enough. There was a note dated All Hallows, 1702, to this effect:

"This day did a vagrant from Elmham beat cruelly to death two poor men who had refused him alms, and upon a hue and cry being raised, took his own life. He was buried in one Parson's Close with a stake through his body and his arms confined in chains, and stoutly covered in."

No further news came from Elmham. Either the effort had been exhausted, or its purpose achieved. But what could have led the young lady, a stranger to Mr. Batchel and to his garden, to hit upon so appropriate a topic? Mr. Batchel could not answer the question as he put it to himself again and again during the day. He only knew that she had given him a warning, by which, to his shame and regret, he had been too obtuse to profit.

The Indian Lampshade

What has been already said of Mr. Batchel will have sufficed to inform the reader that he is a man of very settled habits. The conveniences of life, which have multiplied so fast of late, have never attracted him, even when he has heard of them. Inconveniences to which he is accustomed have always seemed to him preferable to conveniences with which he is unfamiliar. To this day, therefore, he writes with a quill, winds up his watch with a key, and will drink no soda-water but from a tumbling bottle with the cork wired to its neck.

The reader accordingly will learn without surprise that Mr. Batchel continues to use the reading-lamp he acquired thirty years ago as a freshman in college. He still carries it from room to room as occasion requires, and ignores all other means of illumination. It is an inexpensive lamp of very poor appearance, and dates from a time when labour-saving was not yet a fine art. It cannot be lighted without the removal of several of its parts, and it is extinguished by the primitive device of blowing down the chimney. What has always shocked the womenfolk of the Batchel family, however, is the lamp's unworthiness of its surroundings. Mr. Batchel's house is furnished in dignified and comfortable style, but the handsome lamp, surmounting a fluted brazen column, which his relatives bestowed upon him at his institution, is still unpacked.

One of his younger and subtler relatives succeeded in damaging the old lamp, as she thought, irretrievably, by a well-planned accident, but found it still in use a year later, most atrociously repaired. The whole family, and some outsiders, had conspired to attack the offending lamp, and it had withstood them all.

The single victory achieved over Mr. Batchel in this matter is quite recent, and was generally unexpected. A cousin who had gone out to India as a bride, and that of Mr. Batchel's making, had sent him an Indian lampshade. The association was pleasing. The shade was decorated with Buddhist figures which excited Mr. Batchel's curiosity, and to the surprise of all his friends he set it on the lamp and there allowed it to remain. It was not, however, the figures which had reconciled him to this novel and somewhat incongruous addition to the old lamp. The singular colour of the material had really attracted him. It was a bright orange-red, like no colour he had ever seen, and the remarks of visitors whose experience of such things was greater than his own soon justified him in regarding it as unique.

No one had seen the colour elsewhere; and of all the tints which have acquired distinctive names, none of the names could be applied without some further qualification. Mr. Batchel himself did not trouble about a name, but was quite certain that it was a colour that he liked; and more than that, a colour which had about it some indescribable fascination. When the lamp had been brought in, and the curtains drawn, he used to regard with singular pleasure the interiors of rooms with whose appearance he was unaccustomed to concern himself.

The books in his study, and the old-fashioned solid furniture of his dining room, as reflected in the new light, seemed to assume a more friendly aspect, as if they had previously been rigidly frozen, and had now thawed into life. The lampshade seemed to bestow upon the light some active property, and gave to the rooms, as Mr. Batchel said, the appearance of being wide-awake.

These optical effects, as he called them, were especially noticeable in the dining room, where the convenience of a large table often induced him to spend the evening. Standing in a favourite attitude, with his elbow on the chimney-piece, Mr. Batchel found increasing pleasure in contemplating the interior of the room as he saw it reflected in a large old mirror above the fireplace. The great mahogany sideboard across the room, seemed, as he gazed upon it, to be penetrated by the light, and to acquire a softness of outline, and a sort of vivacity, which operated pleasantly upon its owner's imagination. He found himself playfully regretting, for example, that the mirror had no power of recording and reproducing the scenes enacted before it since the close of the 18th century, when it had become one of the fixtures of the house.

The ruddy light of the lamp-shade had always a stimulating effect upon his fancy, and some of the verses which describe his visions before the mirror would delight the reader, but that the author's modesty forbids their reproduction. Had he been less firm in this matter we should have inserted here a poem in which Mr. Batchel audaciously ventured into the domain of physics. He endowed his mirror with the power of retaining indefinitely the light which fell upon it, and of reflecting it only when excited by the appropriate stimulus. The passage beginning

The mirror, whilst men pass upon their way,
Treasures their image for a later day,

might be derided by students of optics. Mr. Batchel has often read it in after days, with amazement, for, when his idle fancies came to be so gravely substantiated, he found that in writing the verses he had stumbled upon a new fact—a fact based as soundly, as will soon appear, upon experiment, as those which the text-books use in arriving at the better-known properties of reflection.

He was seated in his dining room one frosty evening in January. His chair was drawn up to the fire, and the upper part of the space behind him was visible in the mirror. The brighter and clearer light thrown down by the shade was shining upon his book. It is the fate of most of us to receive visits when we should best like to be alone, and Mr. Batchel allowed an impatient exclamation to escape him, when, at nine o'clock on this evening, he heard the door-bell. A minute later, the boy announced "Mr. Mutcher," and Mr. Batchel, with such affability as he could hastily assume, rose to receive the caller. Mr. Mutcher was the Deputy Provincial Grand Master of the Ancient Order of Gleaners, and the formality of his manner accorded with the gravity of his title.

Mr. Batchel soon became aware that the rest of the evening was doomed. The Deputy Provincial Grand Master had come to discuss the probable effect of the Insurance Act upon Friendly Societies, of which Mr. Batchel was an ardent supporter. He attended their meetings, in some cases kept their accounts, and was always apt to be consulted in their affairs. He seated Mr. Mutcher, therefore, in a chair on the opposite side of the fireplace, and gave him his somewhat reluctant attention.

"This," said Mr. Mutcher, as he looked round the room, "is a cosy nook on a cold night. I cordially appreciate your kindness. Reverend Sir, in affording me this interview, and the comfort of your apartment leads me to wish that it might be more protracted."

Mr. Batchel did his best not to dissent, and as he settled himself for a long half-hour, began to watch the rise and fall, between two lines upon the distant wall-paper of the shadow of Mr. Mutcher's side-whisker, as it seemed to beat time to his measured speech.

The D.P.G.M. (for these functionaries are usually designated by initials) was not a man to be hurried into brevity. His style had been studiously acquired at Lodge meetings, and Mr. Batchel knew it well enough to be prepared for a lengthy preamble.

"I have presumed," said Mr. Mutcher, as he looked straight before him into the mirror, "to trespass upon your Reverence's forbearance, because there are one or two points upon this new Insurance Act which seem calculated to damage our long-continued prosperity—I say long-continued prosperity," repeated Mr. Mutcher, as though Mr. Batchel had missed the phrase.

"I had the favour of an interview yesterday," he went on, "with the Sub-Superintendent of the Perseverance Accident and General (these were household words in circles which Mr. Batchel frequented, so that he was at no loss to understand them), and he was unanimous with me in agreeing that the matter called for careful consideration. There are one or two of our rules which we know to be essential to the welfare of our Order, and yet which will have to go by the board—I say by the board—as from July next. Now we are not Medes, nor yet Persians"—Mr. Mutcher was about to repeat "Persians" when he was observed to look hastily round the room and then to turn deadly pale.

Mr. Batchel rose and hastened to his support; he was obviously unwell. The visitor, however, made a strong effort, rose from his chair at once, saying "Pray allow me to take leave," and hurried to the door even as he said the words. Mr. Batchel, with real concern, followed him with the offer of brandy, or whatever might afford relief. Mr. Mutcher did not so much as pause to reply.

Before Mr. Batchel could reach him he had crossed the hall, and the door-knob was in his hand. He thereupon opened the door and passed into the street without another word. More unaccountably still, he went away at a run, such as ill became his somewhat majestic figure, and Mr. Batchel closed the door and returned to the dining-room in a state of bewilderment. He took up his book, and sat down again in his chair. He did not immediately begin to read, but set himself to review Mr. Mutcher's unaccountable behaviour, and as he raised his eyes to the mirror he saw an elderly man standing at the sideboard.

Mr. Batchel quickly turned round, and as he did so, recalled the similar movement of his late visitor. The room was empty. He turned again to the mirror, and the man was still there—evidently a servant—one would say without much hesitation, the butler. The cut-away coat, and white stock, the clean-shaven chin, and close-trimmed side-whiskers, the deftness and decorum of his movements were all characteristic of a respectable family servant, and he stood at the sideboard like a man who was at home there.

Another object, just visible above the frame of the mirror,

caused Mr. Batchel to look round again, and again to see nothing unusual. But what he saw in the mirror was a square oaken box some few inches deep, which the butler was proceeding to unlock. And at this point Mr. Batchel had the presence of mind to make an experiment of extraordinary value. He removed, for a moment, the Indian shade from the lamp, and laid it upon the table, and thereupon the mirror showed nothing but empty space and the frigid lines of the furniture. The butler had disappeared, as also had the box, to reappear the moment the shade was restored to its place.

As soon as the box was opened, the butler produced a bundled handkerchief which his left hand had been concealing under the tails of his coat. With his right hand he removed the contents of the handkerchief, hurriedly placed them in the box, closed the lid, and having done this, left the room at once. His later movements had been those of a man in fear of being disturbed. He did not even wait to lock the box. He seemed to have heard someone coming.

Mr. Batchel's interest in the box will subsequently be explained. As soon as the butler had left, he stood before the mirror and examined it carefully. More than once, as he felt the desire for a closer scrutiny, he turned to the sideboard itself, where of course no box was to be seen, and returned to the mirror unreasonably disappointed. At length, with the image of the box firmly impressed upon his memory, he sat down again in his chair, and reviewed the butler's conduct, or as he doubted he would have to call it, misconduct.

Unfortunately for Mr. Batchel, the contents of the handkerchief had been indistinguishable. But for the butler's alarm, which caused him to be moving away from the box even whilst he was placing the thing within it, the mirror could not have shewn as much as it did. All that had been made evident was that the man had something to conceal, and that it was surreptitiously done.

"Is this all?" said Mr. Batchel to himself as he sat looking into the mirror, "or is it only the end of the first act?" The question was, in a measure, answered by the presence of the box. That, at all events would have to disappear before the room could resume its ordinary aspect; and whether it was to fade out of sight or to be removed by the butler, Mr. Batchel did not intend to be looking another way at the time. He had not seen, although perhaps Mr. Mutcher had, whether the butler had brought it in, but he was determined to see whether he took it out.

He had not gazed into the mirror for many minutes before he learned that there was to be a second act. Quite suddenly, a woman was at the sideboard. She had darted to it, and the time taken in passing over half the length of the mirror had been altogether too brief to show what she was like. She now stood with her face to the sideboard, entirely concealing the box from view, and all Mr. Batchel could determine was that she was tall of stature, and that her hair was raven-black, and not in very good order. In his anxiety to see her face, he called aloud, "Turn round."

Of course, he understood, when he saw that his cry had been absolutely without effect, that it had been a ridiculous thing to do. He turned his head again for a moment to assure himself that the room was empty, and to remind himself that the curtain had fallen, perhaps a century before, upon the drama—he began to think of it as a tragedy—that he was witnessing. The opportunity, however, of seeing the woman's features was not denied him. She turned her face full upon the mirror—this is to speak as if we described the object rather than the image—so that Mr. Batchel saw it plainly before him; it was a handsome, cruel-looking face, of waxen paleness, with fine, distended, lustrous, eyes. The woman looked hurriedly round the room, looked twice towards the door, and then opened the box.

"Our respectable friend was evidently observed," said Mr. Batchel. "If he has annexed anything belonging to this magnificent female, he is in for a bad quarter of an hour." He would have given a great deal, for once, to have had a sideboard backed by a looking glass, and lamented that the taste of the day had been too good to tolerate such a thing. He would have then been able to see what was going on at the oaken box. As it was, the operations were concealed by the figure of the woman. She was evidently busy with her fingers; her elbows, which shewed plainly enough, were vibrating with activity.

In a few minutes there was a final movement of the elbows simultaneously away from her sides, and it shewed, as plainly as if the hands had been visible, that something had been plucked asunder. It was just such a movement as accompanies the removal, after a struggle, of the close-fitting lid of a canister.

"What next?" said Mr. Batchel, as he observed the movement, and interpreted it as the end of the operation at the box. "Is this the end of the second act?"

He was soon to learn that it was not the end, and that the drama of the mirror was indeed assuming the nature of tragedy. The woman closed the box and looked towards the door, as she had done before; then she made as if she would dart out of the room, and found her movement suddenly arrested. She stopped dead, and, in a moment, fell loosely to the ground. Obviously she had swooned away.

Mr. Batchel could then see nothing, except that the box remained in its place on the sideboard, so that he arose and stood close up to the mirror in order to obtain a view of the whole stage, as he called it. It showed him, in the wider view he now obtained, the woman lying in a heap upon the carpet, and a grey-wigged clergyman standing in the doorway of the room.

"The Vicar of Stoneground, without a doubt," said Mr. Batchel. "The household of my reverend predecessor is not doing well by him; to judge from the effect of his appearance upon this female, there's something serious afoot. Poor old man," he added, as the clergyman walked into the room.

This expression of pity was evoked by the vicar's face. The marks of tears were upon his cheeks, and he looked weary and ill. He stood for a while looking down upon the woman who had swooned away, and then stooped down, and gently opened her hand.

Mr. Batchel would have given a great deal to know what the

vicar found there. He took something from her, stood erect for a moment with an expression of consternation upon his face; then his chin dropped, his eyes showed that he had lost consciousness, and he fell to the ground, very much as the woman had fallen.

The two lay, side by side, just visible in the space between the table and the sideboard. It was a curious and pathetic situation. As the clergyman was about to fall, Mr. Batchel had turned to save him, and felt a real distress of helplessness at being reminded again that it was but an image that he had looked upon. The two persons now lying upon the carpet had been for some hundred years beyond human aid. He could no more help them than he could help the wounded at Waterloo. He was tempted to relieve his distress by removing the shade of the lamp; he had even laid his hand upon it, but the feeling of curiosity was now become too strong, and he knew that he must see the matter to its end.

The woman first began to revive. It was to be expected, as she had been the first to go. Had not Mr. Batchel seen her face in the mirror, her first act of consciousness would have astounded him. Now it only revolted him. Before she had sufficiently recovered to raise herself upon her feet, she forced open the lifeless hands beside her and snatched away the contents of that which was not empty; and as she did this, Mr. Batchel saw the glitter of precious stones. The woman was soon upon her feet and making feebly for the door, at which she paused to leer at the prostrate figure of the clergyman before she disappeared into the hall. She appeared no more, and Mr. Batchel felt glad to be rid of her presence.

The old vicar was long in coming to his senses; as he began to move, there stood in the doorway the welcome figure of the butler. With infinite gentleness he raised his master to his feet, and with a strong arm supported him out of the room, which at last, stood empty.

"That, at least," said Mr. Batchel, "is the end of the second act. I doubt whether I could have borne much more. If that awful woman comes back I shall remove the shade and have done with it all. Otherwise, I shall hope to learn what becomes of the box, and whether my respectable friend who has just taken out his master is, or is not, a rascal." He had been genuinely moved by what he had seen, and was conscious of feeling something like exhaustion. He dare not, however, sit down, lest he should lose anything important of what remained. Neither the door nor the lower part of the room was visible from his chair, so that he remained standing at the chimney-piece, and there awaited the disappearance of the oaken box.

So intently were his eyes fixed upon the box, in which he was especially interested, that he all but missed the next incident. A velvet curtain which he could see through the half-closed door had suggested nothing of interest to him. He connected it indefinitely, as it was excusable to do, with the furniture of the house, and only by inadvertence looked at it a second time. When, however, it began to travel slowly along the hall, his curiosity was awakened in a new direction.

The butler, helping his master out of the room ten minutes since, had left the door half open, but as the opening was not towards the mirror, only a strip of the hall beyond could be seen. Mr. Batchel went to open the door more widely, only to find, of course, that the vividness of the images had again betrayed him. The door of his dining-room was closed, as he had closed it after Mr. Mutcher, whose perturbation was now so much easier to understand.

The curtain continued to move across the narrow opening, and explained itself in doing so. It was a pall. The remains it so amply covered were being carried out of the house to their resting-place, and were followed by a long procession of mourners in long cloaks. The hats they held in their black-gloved hands were heavily banded with crepe whose ends descended to the ground, and foremost among them was the old clergyman, refusing the support which two of the chief mourners were in the act of proffering. Mr. Batchel, full of sympathy, watched the whole procession pass the door, and not until it was evident that the funeral had left the house did he turn once more to the box. He felt sure that the closing scene of the tragedy was at hand, and it proved to be very near. It was brief and uneventful. The butler very deliberately entered the room, threw aside the window-curtains and drew up the blinds, and then went away at once, taking the box with him. Mr. Batchel thereupon blew out his lamp and went to bed, with a purpose of his own to be fulfilled upon the next day.

His purpose may be stated at once. He had recognised the oaken box, and knew that it was still in the house. Three large cupboards in the old library of Vicar Whitehead were filled with the papers of a great law-suit about tithe, dating from the close of the 18th century. Amongst these, in the last of the three cupboards, was the box of which so much has been said. It was filled, so far as Mr. Batchel remembered, with the assessments for poor's rate of a large number of landholders concerned in the suit, and these Mr. Batchel had never thought it worth his while to disturb. He had gone to rest, however, on this night with the full intention of going carefully through the contents of the box. He scarcely hoped, after so long an interval, to discover any clue to the scenes he had witnessed, but he was determined at least to make the attempt. If he found nothing, he intended that the box should enshrine a faithful record of the transactions in the dining-room.

It was inevitable that a man who had so much of the material of a story should spend a wakeful hour in trying to piece it together. Mr. Batchel spent considerably more than an hour in connecting, in this way and that, the butler and his master, the gypsy-looking woman, the funeral, but could arrive at no connexion that satisfied him. Once asleep, he found the problem easier, and dreamed a solution so obvious as to make him wonder that the matter had ever puzzled him. When he awoke in the morning, also, the defects of the solution were so obvious as to make him wonder that he had accepted it; so easily are we satisfied when reason is not there to criticise.

But there was still the box, and this Mr. Batchel lifted down from the third cupboard, dusted with his towel, and when he was dressed, carried downstairs with him. His breakfast occupied but a small part of a large table, and upon the vacant area he was soon laying, as he examined them, one by one, the documents which the box contained. His recollection of them proved to be right. They were overseers' lists of parochial assessments, of which he soon had a score or more laid upon the table. They were of no interest in themselves, and did nothing to further the matter in hand. They would appear to have been thrust into the box by someone desiring to find a receptacle for them.

In a little while, however, the character of the papers changed. Mr, Batchel found himself reading something of another kind, written upon paper of another form and colour.

"Irish bacon to be had of Mr. Broadley, hop merchant in Southwark."

"Rasin wine is kept at the Wine and Brandy vaults in Catherine Street."

"The best hones at Mr. Forsters in Little Britain."

There followed a recipe for a "rhumatic mixture," a way of making a polish for mahogany, and other such matters. They were evidently the papers of the butler.

Mr. Batchel removed them one by one, as he had removed the others; household accounts followed, one or two private letters, and the advertisement of a lottery, and then he reached a closed compartment at the bottom of the box, occupying about half its area, The lid of the compartment was provided with a bone stud, and Mr. Batchel lifted it off and laid it upon the table amongst the papers. He saw at once what the butler had taken from his handkerchief. There was an open pocket-knife, with woeful-looking deposits upon its now rusty blade. There was a delicate human finger, now dry and yellow, and on the finger a gold ring,

Mr. Batchel took up this latter pitiful object and removed the ring, even now, not quite easily. He allowed the finger to drop back into the box, which he carried away at once into another room. His appetite for breakfast had left him, and he rang the bell to have the things cleared away, whilst he set himself, with the aid of a lens, to examine the ring.

There had been three large stones, all of which had been violently removed. The claws of their settings were, without exception, either bent outwards, or broken off. Within the ring was engraved, in graceful italic characters, the name *Amey Lee,* and on the broader part, behind the place of the stones

She doth joy double,
And halveth trouble.

This pathetic little love token Mr. Batchel continued to hold in his hand as he rehearsed the whole story to which it afforded the clue. He knew that the ring had been set with such stones as there was no mistaking: he remembered only too well how their discovery had affected the aged vicar. But never would he deny himself the satisfaction of hoping that the old man had been spared the distress of learning how the ring had been removed.

The name of Amey Lee was as familiar to Mr. Batchel as his own. Twice at least every Sunday during the past seven years had he read it at his feet, as he sat in the chancel, as well as the name of Robert Lee upon an adjacent slab, and he had wondered during the leisurely course of many a meandering hymn whether there was good precedent for the spelling of the name. He made another use now of his knowledge of the pavement. There was a row of tiles along the head of the slabs, and Mr. Batchel hastened to fulfil without delay, what he conceived to be his duty. He replaced the ring upon Amey Lee's finger and carried it into the church, and there, having raised one of the tiles with a chisel, gave it decent burial.

Whether the butler ever learned that he had been robbed in his turn, who shall say? His immediate dismissal, after the funeral, seemed inevitable, and his oaken box was evidently placed by him, or by another, where no man heeded it. It still occupies a place amongst the law papers and may lie undisturbed for another century; and when Mr. Batchel put it there, without the promised record of events, he returned to the dining room, removed the Indian shade from the lamp, and, having put a lighted match to the edge, watched it slowly burn away.

Only one thing remained. Mr. Batchel felt that it would give him some satisfaction to visit Mr. Mutcher. His address, as obtained from the District Miscellany of the Order of Gleaners, was 13, Albert Villas, Williamson Street, not a mile away from Stoneground.

Mr. Mutcher, fortunately, was at home when Mr. Batchel called, and indeed opened the door with a copious apology for being without his coat.

"I hope," said Mr. Batchel, "that you have overcome your indisposition of last Tuesday evening."

"Don't mention it, your Reverence," said Mr. Mutcher, "my wife gave me such a talking to when I came 'ome that I was quite ashamed of myself—I say ashamed of myself."

"She observed that you were unwell," said Mr. Batchel, "I am sure; but she could hardly blame you for that."

By this time the visitor had been shewn into the parlour, and Mrs. Mutcher had appeared to answer for herself.

"I really was ashamed, Sir," she said, "to think of the way Mutcher was talking, and a clergyman's 'ouse too. Mutcher is not a man, Sir, that takes anything, not so much as a drop; but he is wonderful partial to cold pork, which never does agree with him, and never did, at night in partic'lar."

"It was the cold pork, then, that made you unwell?" asked Mr. Batchel.

"It was, your Reverence, and it was not," Mr. Mutcher replied, "for internal discomfort there was none—I say none. But a little light-'eaded it did make me, and I could 'ave swore, your Reverence, saving your presence, that I saw an elderly gentleman carry a box into your room and put it down on the sheffoneer."

"There was no one there, of course," observed Mr. Batchel.

"No!" replied the D.P.G.M., "there was not; and the discrepancy was too much for me. I hope you will pardon the abruptness of my departure."

"Certainly," said Mr. Batchel, "discrepancies are always embarrassing."

"And you will allow me one day to resume our discourse upon the subject of National Insurance," he added, when he shewed his visitor to the door.

"I shall not have much leisure," said Mr. Batchel, audaciously, taking all risks, "until the Greek kalends."

"Oh, I don't mind waiting till it does end," said Mr. Mutcher, "there is no immediate 'urry."

"It's rather a long time," remarked Mr. Batchel.

"Pray don't mention it," answered the Deputy Provincial Grand Master, in his best manner. "But when the time comes, perhaps you'll drop me a line."

The Place of Safery

"I thank my governors, teachers, spiritual pastors, and masters," said Wardle, as he lit a cigar after breakfast, "that I never acquired a taste for that sort of thing."

Wardle was a pragmatical and candid friend who paid Mr. Batchel occasional visits at Stoneground. He regarded antiquarian tastes as a form of insanity, and it annoyed him to see his host poring over registers, churchwardens' accounts, and documents which he contemptuously alluded to as "dirty papers." "If you would throw those things away, Batchel," he used to say, "and read the *Daily Mail*, you'd be a better man for it."

Mr. Batchel replied only with a tolerant smile, and, as his friend went out of doors with his cigar, continued to read the document before him, although it was one he had read twenty times before. It was an inventory of church goods, dated the 6th year of Edward VI.—to be exact, the 15th May, 1552. By a royal order of that year, all church goods, saving only what sufficed for the barest necessities of Divine Service, were collected and deposited in safe hands, there to await further instructions. The instructions, which had not been long delayed, had consisted in a court order for seizure. Everyone who cares for such matters, knows and laments the grievous spoliation of those times.

Mr. Batchel's document, however, proved that the churchwardens of the day were not incapable of self-defence. They were less dumb than sheep before the shearers. For, on the copy of the inventory of which he had become possessed, was written the commissioners' report that—

at Stoneground did John Spayn and John Gounthropp, churchwardens, declare upon their othes that two gilded senseres with candellstickes, old paynted clothes, and other implements, were contayned in a chest which was robbed on St. Peter's Eve before the first inventorye made.

Mr. Batchel had a shrewd suspicion, which the reader will not improbably share, that John Spayne and his colleague knew more about the robbery than they chose to admit. He said to himself again and again, that the contents of the chest had been carefully concealed until times should mend. But from the point of view of the churchwardens, times had not mended. There was evidence that Stoneground had been in no mood to tolerate censers in the reign of Mary, and it seemed unlikely that any later time could have readmitted the ancient ritual. On this account, Mr. Batchel had never ceased to believe that the contents of the chest lay somewhere near at hand, nor to hope that it might be his lot to discover it.

Whenever there was any work of the nature of excavation or demolition within a hundred yards of the church, Mr. Batchel was sure to be there. His presence was very distasteful in most cases, to the workmen engaged, whom it deprived of many intervals of leisure to which they were accustomed when left alone. During a long course of operations connected with the restoration of the church, Mr. Batchel's vigilance had been of great advantage to the work, both in raising the standard of industry and in securing attention to details which the builders were quite prepared to overlook. It had, however, brought him no nearer to the censers and other contents of the chest, and when the work was completed, his hopes of discovery had become pitifully slender.

Mr. Wardle, notwithstanding his general contempt for antiquarian pursuits, was polite enough to give Mr. Batchel's hobbies an occasional place in their conversation, and in this way was informed of the "stolen" goods.

The information, however, gave him no more than a very languid interest.

"Why can't you let the things alone?" he said, "what's the use of them?"

Mr. Batchel felt it all but impossible to answer a man who could say this; yet he made the attempt.

"The historic interest," he said seriously, "of censers that were used down to the days of Edward VI. is in itself sufficient to justify—"

"*Etcetera*," said his friend, interrupting the sentence which even Mr. Batchel was not sure of finishing to his satisfaction, "but it takes so little to justify you antiquarians, with your axes and hammers. What can you do with it when you get it, if you ever do get it?"

"There are two censers," Mr. Batchel mildly observed in correction, "and other things."

"All right," said Wardle; "tell me about one of them, and leave me to do the multiplication."

With this permission, Mr. Batchel entered upon a general description of such ancient thuribles as he knew of, and Wardle heard him with growing impatience.

"It seems to me," he burst in at length, "that what you are making all this pother about is a sort of silver cruet-stand, which was thin metal to begin with, and cleaned down to the thickness of egg-shell before the commissioners heard of it. At this moment, if it exists, it is a handful of black scrap. If you found it, I wouldn't give a shilling for it; and if I would, it isn't yours to sell. Why can't you let the things alone?"

"But the interest of it," said Mr. Batchel, "is what attracts me."

"It's a pity you can't take an interest in something less uninteresting," said Wardle, petulantly; "but let me tell you what I think about your censers and all the rest of it. Your churchwardens lied about them, but that's all right; I'd have done the same myself. If their things couldn't be used, they were not going to have them abused, so they put them safely out of the way, your's and everybody's else."

"I was not proposing to abuse them," interrupted Mr. Batchel.

"Were you proposing to use them?" rejoined Wardle. "It's one thing or the other, to my mind. There are people who dig out Bishops and steal their rings to put in glass cases, but I don't know how they square the police; and it's the same sort of thing you seem to be up to. Let the things alone. You're a Prayer Book man, and just the sort the churchwardens couldn't stomach. You talk fast enough at the dissenters because they want to collar your property now. Why can't you do as you would be done by?"

Mr. Batchel thought it useless to say any more to a man in so unsympathetic an attitude, or to enter upon any defence of the antiquarian researches to which his friend had so crudely referred. He did not much like, however, to be anticipated in a theory of the "robbery" which he felt to be reasonable and probable. He had hoped to propound the same theory himself, and to receive a suitable compliment upon his penetration. He began, therefore, somewhat irritably, to make the most of conjectures which, at various times, had occurred to him. "Men of that sort," he said, "would have disposed of the censers to some-one who could go on using them, and in that case they are not here at all."

"Men of that sort," answered Wardle, "are as careful of their skins as men of any other sort, and besides that, your Stone-ground men have a very good notion of sticking to what they have got. The things are here, I daresay, if they are anywhere; but they are not yours, and you have no business to meddle with them. If you would spend your time in something else than poking about after other people's things, you'd get better value for it."

This brief conversation, in which Mr. Batchel had scarce-ly been allowed the part to which he felt entitled, was in one respect satisfactory. It supported his belief that the censers lay somewhere within reach. In other respects, however, the attitude of Wardle was intolerable. He was evidently out of all sympathy with the quest upon which Mr. Batchel was set, and, for their different reasons, each was glad to drop the subject.

During the next two or three days, the matter of the censers was not referred to, if only for lack of opportunity. Wardle was a kind of visitor for whom there was always a welcome at Stoneground, and the welcome was in his case no less cordial on account of his brutal frankness of expression, which, on the whole, his host enjoyed. His pungent criticisms of other men were vastly entertaining to Mr. Batchel, who was not so unreasonable as to feel aggrieved at an occasional attack upon himself.

A guest of this unceremonious sort makes but small demands upon his host. Mr. Wardle used to occupy himself contentedly and unobtrusively in the house or in the garden whilst his host followed his usual avocations. The two men met at meals, and liked each other none the less because they were apart at most other times. A great part of Mr. Wardle's day was passed in the company of the gardener, to whose talk his own master was but an indifferent listener. The visitor and the gardener were both lovers of the soil, and taught each other a great deal as they worked side by side. Mr. Wardle found that sort of exercise wholesome, and, as the gardener expressed it, "was not frit to take his coat off."

The gardening operations at this time of year were such as Mr. Wardle liked. The overcrowded shrubberies were being thinned, and a score or so of young shrubs had to be moved into better quarters. Upon a certain morning, when Mr. Batchel was occupied in his study, some aucubas were being transplanted into a strip of ground in front of the house, and Wardle had undertaken the task of digging holes to receive them. It was this task that he suddenly interrupted in order to burst in upon his host in what seemed to the latter a repulsive state of dirt and perspiration.

"Talk of discoveries," he cried, "come and see what I've found."

"Not the censers, I suppose," said Mr. Batchel.

"Censers be hanged," said Wardle, "come and look."

Mr. Batchel laid down his pen, with a sigh, and followed Wardle to the front of the house His guest had made three large holes, each about two feet square, and drawing Mr. Batchel to the nearest of them, said "Look there."

Mr. Batchel looked. He saw nothing, and said so.

"Nothing?" exclaimed Wardle with impatience. "You see the bottom of the hole, I suppose?"

This Mr. Batchel admitted.

"Then," said Wardle, "kindly look and see whether you cannot see something else."

"There is apparently a cylindrical object lying across the angle of your excavation," said Mr. Batchel.

"That," replied his guest, "is what you are pleased to call nothing. Let me inform you that the cylindrical object is a piece of thick lead pipe, and that the pipe runs along the whole front of your house."

"Gas-pipe, no doubt," said Mr. Batchel.

"Is there any gas within a mile of this place?" asked Wardle.

Mr. Batchel admitted that there was not, and felt that he had made a needlessly foolish suggestion. He felt safer in the amended suggestion that the object was a water-pipe.

An ironical cross-examination by Mr. Wardle disposed of the amended suggestion as completely as he had disposed of the other, and his host began to grow restive. "If this sort of discovery pleases you," he said testily, "I will not grudge you your pleasure, but, to quote your own words, why can't you let it alone?"

"Have you any idea," said Mr. Wardle, "of the value of this length of piping, at the present price of lead?"

Even Mr. Wardle could hardly have suspected his host of knowing anything so preposterous as the price of lead, but he felt himself ill-used when Mr. Batchel disclaimed any interest in the matter, and returned to his study.

Wardle had a commercial mind, which elsewhere was the means of securing him a very satisfactory income, and on this account, his host, as he resumed his work indoors, excused what he regarded as a needless interruption.

He little suspected that his friend's commercial mind was to do him the great service of putting him in possession of the censers, and then to do him a disservice even greater.

Had any such connexion so much as suggested itself, Mr. Batchel would more willingly have answered to the summons which came an hour later, when the gardener appeared at the window of the study, evidently bursting with information. When he had succeeded in attracting his master's attention, and drawn him away from his desk, it was to say that the whole length of pipe had been uncovered, and found to issue from a well on the south side of the house.

The discovery was at least unexpected, and Mr. Batchel went out, even if somewhat grudgingly, to look at the place. He came upon the well, close by the window of his dining-room. It had been covered by a stone slab, now partially removed. The narrow trench which Wardle and the gardener had made in order to expose the pipe, extended eastwards to the corner of the house, and thence along the whole length of the front, probably to serve a pump on the north side, where lay the yard and stables. The pipe itself, Mr. Wardle's prize, had been withdrawn, and there remained only a rusted chain which passed from some anchorage beneath the soil, over the lip of the well. Mr. Batchel inferred that it had carried, and perhaps carried still, the bucket of former times, and stooped down to see whether he could draw it up. He heard, far below, the light splash of the soil disturbed by his hands; but before he could grasp the chain, he felt himself seized by the waist and held back.

The exaggerated attentions of his gardener had often annoyed Mr. Batchel. He was not allowed even to climb a short ladder without having to submit to absurd precautions for his safety, and he would have been much better pleased to have more respect paid to his intelligence, and less to his person. In the present instance, the precaution seemed so unnecessary that he turned about angrily to protest, both against the interference with his movements, and the unseemly force used.

It was at this point that he made a disquieting discovery. He was standing quite alone. The gardener and Mr. Wardle were both on the north side of the house, dealing with the only thing they cared about—the lead pipe. Mr. Batchel made no further attempt to move the chain; he was, in fact, in some bodily fear, and he returned to his study by the way he had come, in a disordered condition of mind.

Half an hour later, when the gong sounded for luncheon, he was slowly making his way into the dining-room, when he encountered his guest running downstairs from his room, in great spirits. "A trifle over two hundred weight!" he exclaimed, as he reached the foot of the staircase, and seemed disappointed that Mr. Batchel did not immediately shake hands with him upon so fine a result of the morning's work. Mr. Batchel, needless to say, was occupied with other recollections.

"I suppose it is unnecessary to ask," said he to his guest as he proceeded to carve a chicken, "whether you believe in ghosts?"

"I do not," said Wardle promptly, "why should I?"

"Why not?" asked Mr. Batchel.

"Because I've had the advantage of a commercial education," was the reply, "instead of learning dead languages and soaking my mind in heathen fables."

Mr. Batchel winced at this disrespectful allusion to the University education of which he was justly proud. He wanted an opinion, however, and the conversation had to go on.

"Your commercial education," he continued, "allows you, I daresay, to know what is meant by a hypothetical case."

"Make it one," said Wardle.

"Assuming a ghost, then, would it be capable of exerting force upon a material body? "

"Whose? "asked Wardle.

"If you insist upon making it a personal matter," replied Mr. Batchel, "let us say mine."

"Let me have the particulars."

In reply to this, Mr. Batchel related his experience at the well.

Mr. Wardle merely said "Pass the salt, I need it."

Undeterred by the scepticism of his friend, Mr. Batchel pressed the point, and upon that, Mr. Wardle closed the conversation by observing that since, by hypothesis, ghosts could clank chains, and ring bells, he was bound to suppose them capable of doing any silly thing they chose. "A month in the city, Batchel," he gravely added, "would do you a world of good."

As soon as the meal was over, Mr. Wardle went back to his gardening, whilst his host betook himself to occupations more suited to his tranquil habits. The two did not meet again until dinner; and during that meal, and after it, the conversation turned wholly upon politics, Mr. Wardle being congenially occupied until bedtime in demonstrating that the politics of his host had been obsolete for three-quarters of a century. His outdoor exercise, followed by an excellent dinner, had disposed him to retire early; he rose from his chair soon after ten. "There is one thing," he pleasantly remarked to his host, "that I am bound to say in favour of a university education; it has given you a fine taste in victuals." With this compliment, he said "goodnight," and went up to bed.

Mr. Batchel himself, as the reader knows, kept later hours. There were few nights upon which he omitted to take his walk round the garden when the world had grown quiet, even in unfavourable weather. It was far from favourable upon the present occasion; there was but little moon, and a light rain was falling. He determined, however, to take at least one turn round, and calling his terrier Punch from the kitchen, where he lay in his basket, Mr. Batchel went out, with the dog at his heel. He carried, as his custom was, a little electric lamp, by whose aid he liked to peep into birds' nests, and make raids upon slugs and other pests.

They had hardly set out upon their walk when Punch began to show signs of uneasiness. Instead of running to and fro, with his nose to the ground, as he ordinarily did, the terrier remained whining in the rear. Shortly, they came upon a hedgehog lying coiled up in the path; it was a find which the dog was wont to regard as a rare piece of luck, and to assail with delirious enjoyment. Now, for some reason. Punch refused to notice it, and, when it was illuminated for his especial benefit, turned his back upon it and looked up, in a dejected attitude, at his master.

The behaviour of the dog was altogether unnatural, and Mr. Batchel occupied himself, as they passed on, in trying to account for it, with the animal still whining at his heel. They soon reached the head of the little path which descended to the Lode, and there Mr. Batchel found a much harder problem awaiting him, for at the other end of the path he distinctly saw the outline of a boat.

There had been no boat on the Lode for twenty years. Just so long ago the drainage of the district had required that the main sewer should cross the stream at a point some hundred yards below the Vicar's boundary fence. There, ever since, a great pipe three feet in diameter had obstructed the passage. It lay just at the level of the water, and effectually closed it to all traffic. Mr. Batchel knew that no boat could pass the place, and that none survived in the parts above it. Yet here was a boat drawn up at the edge of his garden. He looked at it intently for a minute or so, and had no difficulty in making out the form of such a boat as was in common use all over the Fen country—a wide flat-bottomed boat, lying low in the water.

The "sprit" used for punting it along lay projecting over the stern. There was no accounting for such a boat being there: Mr. Batchel did not understand how it possibly could be there, and for a while was disposed to doubt whether it actually was. The great drain-pipe was so perfect a defence against intrusion of the kind that no boat had ever passed it. The Lode, when its water was low enough to let a boat go under the pipe, was not deep enough to float it, or wide enough to contain it. Upon this occasion the water was high, and the pipe half submerged, forming an insuperable obstacle. Yet there lay, unmistakeably, a boat, within ten yards of the place where Mr. Batchel stood trying to account for it.

These ten yards, unfortunately, were impassable. The slope down to the water's edge had to be warily trodden even in dry weather. It was steep and treacherous. After rain it afforded no foothold whatever, and to attempt a descent in the darkness would have been to court disaster. After examining the boat again, therefore, by the light of his little lamp, Mr. Batchel proceeded upon his walk, leaving the matter to be investigated by daylight.

The events of this memorable night, however, were but beginning. As he turned from the boat his eye was caught by a white streak upon the ground before him, which extended itself into the darkness and disappeared. It was Punch, in veritable panic, making for home, across flower-beds and other places he well knew to be out of bounds. The whistle he had been trained to obey had no effect upon his flight; he made a lightning dash for the house. Mr. Batchel could not help regretting that Wardle was not there to see.

His friend held the coursing powers of Punch in great contempt, and was wont to criticise the dog in sporting jargon, whose terms lay beyond the limits of Mr. Batchers vocabulary, but whose general drift was as obvious as it was irritating. The present performance, nevertheless, was so exceptional that it soon began to connect itself in Mr. Batchel's mind with the unnatural conduct to which we have already alluded. It was somehow proving to be an uncomfortable night, and as Mr. Batchel felt the rain increasing to a steady drizzle he decided to abandon his walk and to return to the house by the way he had come.

He had already passed some little distance beyond the little path which descended to the Lode. The main path by which he had come was of course behind him, until he turned about to retrace his steps.

It was at the moment of turning that he had ocular demonstration of the fact that the boat had brought passengers. Not twenty yards in front of him, making their way to the water, were two men carrying some kind of burden. They had reached an open space in the path, and their forms were quite distinct: they were unusually tall men; one of them was gigantic. Mr. Batchel had little doubt of their being garden thieves. Burglars, if there had been anything in the house to attract them, could have found much easier ways of removing it.

No man, even if deficient in physical courage, can see his

property carried away before his eyes and make no effort to detain it. Mr. Batchel was annoyed at the desertion of his terrier, who might at least have embarrassed the thieves' retreat; meanwhile he called loudly upon the men to stand, and turned upon them the feeble light of his lamp. In so doing he threw a new light not only upon the trespassers, lout upon the whole transaction. No response was made to his challenge, hut the men turned away their faces as if to avoid recognition, and Mr. Batchel saw that the nearest of them, a burly, square-headed man in a cassock, was wearing the tonsure. He described it as looking, in the dim, steely light of the lamp, like a crown-piece on a doormat.

Both the men, when they found themselves intercepted, hastened to deposit their burden upon the ground, and made for the boat. The burden fell upon the ground with a thud, but the bearers made no sound. They skimmed down to the Lode without seeming to tread, entered the boat in perfect silence, and shoved it off without sound or splash. It has already been explained that Mr. Batchel was unable to descend to the water's edge. He ran, however, to a point of the garden which the boat must inevitably pass, and reached it just in time.

The boat was moving swiftly away, and still in perfect silence. The beams of the pocket-lamp just sufficed to reach it, and afforded a parting glimpse of the tonsured giant as he gave a long shove with the sprit, and carried the boat out of sight. It shot towards the drain-pipe, then not forty yards ahead, but the men were travelling as men who knew their way to be clear.

It was by this time evident, of course, that these were no garden-thieves. The aspect of the men, and the manner of their disappearance, had given a new complexion to the adventure. Mr. Batchel's heart was in his mouth, but his mind was back in the 16th century; and having stood still for some minutes in order to regain his composure, he returned to the path, with a view of finding out what the men had left behind.

The burden lay in the middle of the path, and the lamp was once more brought into requisition. It revealed a wooden box, covered in most parts with moss, and all glistening with moisture. The wood was so far decayed that Mr. Batchel had hopes of forcing open the box with his hands; so wet and slimy was it, however, that he could obtain no hold, and he hastened to the house to procure some kind of tool.

Near to the cupboard in which such things were kept was the sleeping-basket of the dog, who was closely curled inside it, and shivering violently. His master made an attempt to take him back into the garden; it would be useful, he thought, to have warning in case the boat should return. The prospect of being surprised by these large, noiseless men was not one to be regarded with comfort. Punch, however, who was usually so eager for an excursion, was now in such distress at being summoned that his master felt it cruel to persist. Having found a chisel, therefore, he returned to the garden alone. The box lay undisturbed where he had left it, and in two minutes was standing open.

The reader will hardly need to be told what it contained. At the bottom lay some heavy articles which Mr. Batchel did not disturb. He saw the bases of two candlesticks. He had tried to lift the box, as it lay, by means of a chain passing through two handles in the sides, but had found it too heavy. It was by this chain that the men had been carrying it. The heavier articles, therefore, he determined to leave where they were until morning. His interest in them was small compared with that which the other contents of the box had excited, for on the top of these articles was folded "a paynted cloth," and upon this lay the two gilded censers.

It was the discovery Mr. Batchel had dreamed of for years. His excitement hardly allowed him to think of the strange manner in which it had been made. He glanced nervously around him, to see whether there might be any sign of the occupants of the boat, and, seeing nothing, he placed his broad-brimmed hat upon the ground, carefully laid in it the two censers, closed the box again, and carried his treasure delicately into the house. The occurrences of the last hour have not occupied long in the telling; they occupied much longer in the happening.

It was now past midnight, and Mr. Batchel, after making fast the house, went at once upstairs, carrying with him the hat and its precious contents, just as he had brought it from the garden. The censers were not exactly "black-scrap," as Mr. Wardle had anticipated, or pretended to anticipate, but they were much discoloured, and very fragile. He spread a clean handkerchief upon the chest of drawers in his bedroom, and, removing the vessels with the utmost care, laid them upon it. Then after spending some minutes in admiration of their singularly beautiful form and workmanship, he could not deny himself the pleasure of calling Wardle to look.

The guest-room was close at hand. Mr. Wardle, having been already disturbed by the locking up of the house, was fully awakened by the entrance of his host into the room with a candle in his hand. The look of excitement on Mr. Batchel's face could not escape the observation even of a man still yawning, and Mr. Wardle at once exclaimed "What's up?"

"I have got them," said Mr. Batchel, in a hushed voice.

His guest, who had forgotten all about the censers, began by interpreting "them" to mean a nervous disorder that is plural by nature, and so was full of sympathy and counsel. When, however, his host had made him understand the facts, he became merely impatient.

"Won't you come and look?" said Mr. Batchel.

"Not I," said Wardle, "I shall do where I am."

"They are in excellent preservation," said Mr. Batchel.

"Then they will keep till morning," was the answer.

"But just come and tell me what you think of them," said Mr. Batchel, making a last attempt.

"I could tell you what I think of them," answered Wardle, "without leaving my bed, which I have no intention of leaving; but I have to leave Stoneground tomorrow, and I don't want to hurt your feelings, so "Goodnight." Upon this, he turned over in bed and gave a loud snore, which Mr. Batchel accepted as a manifesto. He has never ceased to regret that he did not compel his guest to see the censers, but he did not then foresee the sore need he would have of a witness. He answered his friend's goodnight, and returned to his own room.

Once more he admired the two censers as their graceful out-lines stood out, sharp and clear, against the white handkerchief, and having done this, he was soon in bed and asleep. To the men in the boat he had not given another thought, since he became possessed of the box they had left behind; of the other contents of the box he had thought as little, since he had secured the chief treasures of which he had been so long in search.

Now, Mr. Wardle, when he arose in the morning, felt some-what ashamed of his surliness of the preceding night. His repu-diation of all interest in the censers had not been quite sincere, for beneath his affectation of unconcern there lay a genuine curiosity about his friend's discovery. Before he had finished dressing, therefore, he crossed over into Mr. Batchel's room. The censers, to his surprise, were nowhere to be seen.

His host, less to his surprise, was still fast asleep. Mr. Wardle opened the drawers, one by one, in search of the censers, but the drawers proved to be all quite full of clothing. He looked with no more success into every other place where they might have been bestowed. His mind was always ready with a grotesque idea, "Blest if he hasn't taken them to bed with him," he said aloud, and at the sound of his voice Mr. Batchel awoke.

His eyes, as soon as they were open, turned to the chest of drawers; and what he saw there, or rather, what he failed to see, caused him, without more ado, to leap out of bed.

"What have you done with them?" he cried out.

The serious alarm of Mr. Batchel was so evident as to check the facetious reply which Wardle was about to frame. He con-tented himself with saying that he had not touched or seen the things.

"Where are they?" again cried Mr. Batchel, ignoring the dis-claimer. "You ought not to have touched them, they will not bear handling. Where are they?"

Mr. Wardle turned away in disgust, "I expect," he said, "they're where they've been this three hundred and fifty years." Upon that he returned to his room, and went on with his dressing.

Mr. Batchel immediately followed him, and looked eagerly round the room. He proceeded to open drawers, and to search, in a frenzied manner, in every possible, and in many an impossible, place of concealment. His distress was so patent that his friend soon ceased to trifle with it. By a few minutes serious conversation he made it clear that there had been no practical joking, and Mr. Batchel returned to his room in tears. "Look here, Batchel," said Mr. Wardle as he left, "you want a holiday."

Within a few minutes Mr. Batchel returned fully dressed. "You seem to think, Wardle," he said, "that I have been dreaming about these censers. Come out into the garden and let me shew you the box and the other things."

Mr. Wardle was quite willing to assent to anything, if only out of pity, and the two went together into the garden, Mr. Batchel leading the way. Going at a great pace, they soon came to the path upon which the box had lain. The marks it had left upon the soft gravel were plain enough, and Mr. Batchel eagerly appealed to his friend to notice them. Of the box and its contents, however, there was no other trace. The whole adventure was described—the strange behaviour and subsequent flight of the terrier—the men with averted faces—the boat—and the opening of the box. Mr. Batchel tried to shake the, obvious incredulity of his guest by pointing to the chisel which still lay beside the path. Mr. Wardle only replied, "You want a holiday, Batchel! Let's go in to breakfast."

Breakfast on that morning was not the cheerful meal it was wont to be. During the few minutes of waiting for it Mr. Batchel stood at the window of his dining-room looking out upon the site of the well which the gardener had now covered in. He rehearsed the whole of the adventure from first to last, wondering whether the new place of safety would ever be discovered. But he said no more to his guest; his heart was too full.

The two breakfasted almost in silence, and the meal was scarcely over when the cab arrived to take Mr. Wardle to his train. Mr. Batchel bade him farewell, and saw him depart with genuine regret; he was returning sadly into the house when he heard his name called. It was Wardle, leaning out of the window of his cab as it drove away, and waving his hand, "Batchel," he cried again, "mind you take a holiday."

The Kirk Spook

Before many years have passed it will be hard to find a person who has ever seen a parish clerk. The parish clerk is all but extinct. Our grandfathers knew him well—an oldish, clean-shaven man, who looked as if he had never been young, who dressed in rusty black, bestowed upon him, as often as not by the rector, and who usually wore a white tie on Sundays, out of respect for the seriousness of his office. He it was who laid out the rector's robes, and helped him to put them on; who found the places in the large Bible and Prayer Book, and indicated them by means of decorous silken book-markers; who lighted and snuffed the candles in the pulpit and desk, and attended to the little stove in the squire's pew; who ran busily about, in short, during the quarter-hour which preceded Divine Service, doing a hundred little things, with all the activity, and much of the appearance, of a beetle.

Just such a one was Caleb Dean, who was Clerk of Stoneground in the days of William IV. Small in stature, he possessed a voice which nature seemed to have meant for a giant, and in the discharge of his duties he had a dignity of manner disproportionate even to his voice. No one was afraid to sing when he led the psalm, so certain was it that no other voice could be noticed, and the gracious condescension with which he received his meagre fees would have been ample acknowledgment of double their amount.

Man, however, cannot live by dignity alone, and Caleb was glad enough to be sexton as well as clerk, and to undertake any other duties by which he might add to his modest income. He kept the churchyard tidy, trimmed the lamps, chimed the bells, taught the choir their simple tunes, turned the barrel of the organ, and managed the stoves.

It was this last duty in particular, which took him into church "last thing," as he used to call it, on Saturday night. There were people in those days, and may be some in these, whom nothing would induce to enter a church at midnight; Caleb, however, was so much at home there that all hours were alike to him. He was never an early man on Saturdays. His wife, who insisted upon sitting up for him, would often knit her way into Sunday before he appeared, and even then would find it hard to get him to bed. Caleb, in fact, when off duty, was a genial little fellow; he had many friends, and on Saturday evenings he knew where to find them.

It was not, therefore, until the evening was spent that he went to make up his fires; and his voice, which served for other singing than that of psalms, could usually be heard, within a little of midnight, beguiling the way to church with snatches of convivial songs. Many a belated traveller, homeward bound, would envy him his spirits, but no one envied him his duties. Even such as walked with him to the neighbourhood of the churchyard would bid him "Goodnight" whilst still a long way from the gate. They would see him disappear into the gloom amongst the graves, and shudder as they turned homewards.

Caleb, meanwhile, was perfectly content. He knew every stone in the path; long practice enabled him, even on the darkest night, to thrust his huge key into the lock at the first attempt, and on the night we are about to describe—it had come to Mr. Batchel from an old man who heard it from Caleb's lips—he did it with a feeling of unusual cheerfulness and contentment.

Caleb always locked himself in. A prank had once been played upon him, which had greatly wounded his dignity; and though it had been no midnight prank, he had taken care, ever since, to have the church to himself. He locked the door, therefore, as usual, on the night we speak of, and made his way to the stove.

He used no candle. He opened the little iron door of the stove, and obtained sufficient light to shew him the fuel he had laid in readiness; then, when he had made up his fire, he closed this door again, and left the church in darkness. He never could say what induced him upon this occasion to remain there after his task was done. He knew that his wife was sitting up, as usual, and that, as usual, he would have to hear what she had to say. Yet, instead of making his way home, he sat down in the comer of the nearest seat. He supposed that he must have felt tired, but had no distinct recollection of it.

The church was not absolutely dark. Caleb remembered that he could make out the outlines of the windows, and that through the window nearest to him he saw a few stars. After his eyes had grown accustomed to the gloom he could see the lines of the seats taking shape in the darkness, and he had not long sat there before he could dimly see everything there was. At last he began to distinguish where books lay upon the shelf in front of him. And then he closed his eyes. He does not admit having fallen asleep, even for a moment. But the seat was restful, the neighbouring stove was growing warm, he had been through a long and joyous evening, and it was natural that he should at least close his eyes.

He insisted that it was only for a moment. Something, he could not say what, caused him to open his eyes again immediately. The closing of them seemed to have improved what may be called his dark sight. He saw everything in the church quite distinctly, in a sort of grey light. The pulpit stood out, large and bulky, in front. Beyond that, he passed his eyes along the four windows on the north side of the church. He looked again at the stars, still visible through the nearest window on his left hand as he was sitting. From that, his eyes fell to the further end of the seat in front of him, where he could even see a faint gleam of polished wood. He traced this gleam to the middle of the seat, until it disappeared in black shadow, and upon that his eye passed on to the seat he was in, and there he saw a man sitting beside him.

Caleb described the man very clearly. He was, he said, a pale, old-fashioned looking man, with something very churchy about him. Reasoning also with great clearness, he said that the stranger had not come into the church either with him or after him, and that therefore he must have been there before him. And in that case, seeing that the church had been locked since two in the afternoon, the stranger must have been there for a considerable time.

Caleb was puzzled; turning therefore, to the stranger, he asked "How long have you been here?"

The stranger answered at once "Six hundred years."

"Oh! come!" said Caleb.

"Come where?" said the stranger.

"Well, if you come to that, come out," said Caleb.

"I wish I could," said the stranger, and heaved a great sigh.

"What's to prevent you?" said Caleb. "There's the door, and here's the key."

"That's it," said the other.

"Of course it is," said Caleb. "Come along."

With that he proceeded to take the stranger by the sleeve, and then it was that he says you might have knocked him down with a feather. His hand went right into the place where the sleeve seemed to be, and Caleb distinctly saw two of the stranger's buttons on the top of his own knuckles.

He hastily withdrew his hand, which began to feel icy cold, and sat still, not knowing what to say next. He found that the stranger was gently chuckling with laughter, and this annoyed him."

"What are you laughing at?" he enquired peevishly.

"It's not funny enough for two," answered the other.

"Who are you, anyhow?" said Caleb.

"I am the kirk spook," was the reply.

Now Caleb had not the least notion what a "kirk spook" was. He was not willing to admit his ignorance, but his curiosity was too much for his pride, and he asked for information.

"Every church has a spook," said the stranger, "and I am the

119

spook of this one."

"Oh," said Caleb, "I've been about this church a many years, but I've never seen you before."

"That," said the spook, "is because you've always been moving about. I'm very flimsy—very flimsy indeed—and I can only keep myself together when everything is quite still."

"Well," said Caleb, "you've got your chance now. What are you going to do with it?"

"I want to go out," said the spook, "I'm tired of this church, and I've been alone for six hundred years. It's a long time."

"It does seem rather a long time," said Caleb, "but why don't you go if you want to? There's three doors."

"That's just it," said the spook, "They keep me in."

"What?" said Caleb, "when they're open."

"Open or shut," said the spook, "it's all one."

"Well, then," said Caleb, "what about the windows?"

"Every bit as bad," said the spook, "They're all pointed."

Caleb felt out of his depth. Open doors and windows that kept a person in—if it was a person—seemed to want a little understanding. And the flimsier the person, too, the easier it ought to be for him to go where he wanted. Also, what could it matter whether they were pointed or not?

The latter question was the one which Caleb asked first.

"Six hundred years ago," said the spook, "all arches were made round, and when these pointed things came in I cursed them. I hate new-fangled things."

"That wouldn't hurt them much," said Caleb.

"I said I would never go under one of them," said the spook.

"That would matter more to you than to them," said Caleb.

"It does," said the spook, with another great sigh.

"But you could easily change your mind," said Caleb.

"I was tied to it," said the spook, "I was told that I never more should go under one of them, whether I would or not."

"Some people will tell you anything," answered Caleb.

"It was a bishop," explained the spook.

"Ah!" said Caleb, "that's different, of course."

The spook told Caleb how often he had tried to go under the pointed arches, sometimes of the doors, sometimes of the windows, and how a stream of wind always struck him from the point of the arch, and drifted him back into the church. He had long given up trying.

"You should have been outside," said Caleb, "before they built the last door."

"It was my church," said the spook, "and I was too proud to leave."

Caleb began to sympathise with the spook. He had a pride in the church himself, and disliked even to hear another person say Amen before him. He also began to be a little jealous of this stranger who had been six hundred years in possession of the church, in which Caleb had believed himself, under the vicar, to be master. And he began to plot.

"Why do you want to get out?" he asked.

"I'm no use here," was the reply, "I don't get enough to do to keep myself warm. And I know there are scores of churches now without any kirk spooks at all. I can hear their cheap little bells dinging every Sunday."

"There's very few bells hereabouts," said Caleb.

"There's no hereabouts for spooks," said the other. "We can hear any distance you like."

"But what good are you at all?" said Caleb.

"Good!" said the spook. "Don't we secure proper respect for churches, especially after dark? A church would be like any other place if it wasn't for us. You must know that."

"Well, then," said Caleb, "you're no good here. This church is all right. What will you give me to let you out?"

"Can you do it?" asked the spook.

"What will you give me?" said Caleb.

"I'll say a good word for you amongst the spooks," said the other.

"What good will that do me?" said Caleb.

"A good word never did anybody any harm yet," answered

121

the spook.

"Very well then, come along," said Caleb.

"Gently then," said the spook; "don't make a draught."

"Not yet," said Caleb, and he drew the spook very carefully (as one takes a vessel quite full of water) from the seat.

"I can't go under pointed arches," cried the spook, as Caleb moved off.

"Nobody wants you to," said Caleb. "Keep close to me."

He led the spook down the aisle to the angle of the wall where a small iron shutter covered an opening into the flue. It was used by the chimney sweep alone, but Caleb had another use for it now. Calling to the spook to keep close, he suddenly removed the shutter.

The fires were by this time burning briskly. There was a strong up-draught as the shutter was removed. Caleb felt something rush across his face, and heard a cheerful laugh away up in the chimney. Then he knew that he was alone. He replaced the shutter, gave another look at his stoves, took the keys, and made his way home.

He found his wife asleep in her chair, sat down and took off his boots, and awakened her by throwing them across the kitchen.

"I've been wondering when you'd wake," he said.

"What?" she said, "Have you been in long?"

"Look at the clock," said Caleb. "Half after twelve."

"My gracious," said his wife. "Let's be off to bed."

"Did you tell her about the spook?" he was naturally asked.

"Not I," said Caleb. "You know what she'd say. Same as she always does of a Saturday night."

★ ★ ★ ★ ★ ★

This fable Mr. Batchel related with reluctance. His attitude towards it was wholly deprecatory. Psychic phenomena, he said, lay outside the province of the mere humorist, and the levity with which they had been treated was largely responsible for the presumptuous materialism of the age.

He said more, as he warmed to the subject, than can here be repeated. The reader of the foregoing tales, however, will be interested to know that Mr. Batchel's own attitude was one of humble curiosity. He refused even to guess why the *revenant* was sometimes invisible, and at other times partly or wholly visible; sometimes capable of using physical force, and at other times powerless. He knew that they had their periods, and that was all.

There is room, he said, for the romancer in these matters; but for the humorist, none. Romance was the play of intelligence about the confines of truth. The invisible world, like the visible, must have its romancers, its explorers, and its interpreters; but the time of the last was not yet come.

Criticism, he observed in conclusion, was wholesome and necessary. But of the idle and mischievous remarks which were wont to pose as criticism, he held none in so much contempt as the cheap and irrational Pooh-Pooh.

Black Spirits and White

Ralph Adams Cram

Contents

No. 252 Rue M. le Prince   131

In Kropfsberg Keep   147

The White Villa   158

Sister Maddelena   172

Notre Dame des Eaux   189

The Dead Valley   197

Postscript   207

BLACK SPIRITS AND WHITE,
RED SPIRITS AND GRAY,
MINGLE, MINGLE, MINGLE,
YE THAT MINGLE MAY.

No. 252 Rue M. le Prince

When in May, 1886, I found myself at last in Paris, I naturally determined to throw myself on the charity of an old chum of mine, Eugene Marie d'Ardeche, who had forsaken Boston a year or more ago on receiving word of the death of an aunt who had left him such property as she possessed. I fancy this windfall surprised him not a little, for the relations between the aunt and nephew had never been cordial, judging from Eugene's remarks touching the lady, who was, it seems, a more or less wicked and witch-like old person, with a penchant for black magic, at least such was the common report.

Why she should leave all her property to d'Ardeche, no one could tell, unless it was that she felt his rather hobbledehoy tendencies towards Buddhism and occultism might some day lead him to her own unhallowed height of questionable illumination. To be sure d'Ardeche reviled her as a bad old woman, being himself in that state of enthusiastic exaltation which sometimes accompanies a boyish fancy for occultism; but in spite of his distant and repellent attitude, Mlle. Blaye de Tartas made him her sole heir, to the violent wrath of a questionable old party known to infamy as the Sar Torrevieja, the "King of the Sorcerers."

This malevolent old portent, whose gray and crafty face was often seen in the Rue M. le Prince during the life of Mlle. de Tartas had, it seems, fully expected to enjoy her small wealth after her death; and when it appeared that she had left him only the contents of the gloomy old house in the Quartier Latin, giving the house itself and all else of which she died possessed to her nephew in America, the *Sar* proceeded to remove everything from the place, and then to curse it elaborately and comprehensively, together with all those who should ever dwell therein.

Whereupon he disappeared.

This final episode was the last word I received from Eugene, but I knew the number of the house, 252 Rue M. le Prince. So, after a day or two given to a first cursory survey of Paris, I started across the Seine to find Eugene and compel him to do the honours of the city.

Everyone who knows the Latin Quarter knows the Rue M. le Prince, running up the hill towards the Garden of the Luxembourg. It is full of queer houses and odd corners,—or was in '86,—and certainly No. 252 was, when I found it, quite as queer as any. It was nothing but a doorway, a black arch of old stone between and under two new houses painted yellow. The effect of this bit of seventeenth-century masonry, with its dirty old doors, and rusty broken lantern sticking gaunt and grim out over the narrow sidewalk, was, in its frame of fresh plaster, sinister in the extreme.

I wondered if I had made a mistake in the number; it was quite evident that no one lived behind those cobwebs. I went into the doorway of one of the new *hôtels* and interviewed the concierge.

No, M. d'Ardeche did not live there, though to be sure he owned the mansion; he himself resided in Meudon, in the country house of the late Mlle. de Tartas. Would *Monsieur* like the number and the street?

Monsieur would like them extremely, so I took the card that the concierge wrote for me, and forthwith started for the river, in order that I might take a steamboat for Meudon. By one of those coincidences which happen so often, being quite inexplicable, I had not gone twenty paces down the street before I ran directly into the arms of Eugene d'Ardeche. In three minutes we were sitting in the queer little garden of the Chien Bleu, drinking vermouth and absinthe, and talking it all over.

"You do not live in your aunt's house?" I said at last, interrogatively.

"No, but if this sort of thing keeps on I shall have to. I like Meudon much better, and the house is perfect, all furnished, and nothing in it newer than the last century. You must come out with me to-night and see it. I have got a jolly room fixed up for my Buddha. But there is something wrong with this house opposite. I can't keep a tenant in it,—not four days. I have had three, all within six months, but the stories have gone around and a man would as soon think of hiring the Cour des Comptes to live in as No. 252. It is notorious. The fact is, it is haunted the worst way."

I laughed and ordered more vermouth.

"That is all right. It is haunted all the same, or enough to keep it empty, and the funny part is that no one knows *how* it is haunted. Nothing is ever seen, nothing heard. As far as I can find out, people just have the horrors there, and have them so bad they have to go to the hospital afterwards. I have one ex-tenant in the Bicêtre now. So the house stands empty, and as it covers considerable ground and is taxed for a lot, I don't know what to do about it. I think I'll either give it to that child of sin, Torrevieja, or else go and live in it myself. I shouldn't mind the ghosts, I am sure."

"Did you ever stay there?"

"No, but I have always intended to, and in fact I came up here today to see a couple of rake-hell fellows I know, Fargeau and Duchesne, doctors in the Clinical Hospital beyond here, up by the Parc Mont Souris. They promised that they would spend the night with me some time in my aunt's house,—which is called around here, you must know, '*la Bouche d'Enfer*,'—and I thought perhaps they would make it this week, if they can get off duty. Come up with me while I see them, and then we can go across the river to Véfour's and have some luncheon, you can get your things at the Chatham, and we will go out to Meudon, where of course you will spend the night with me."

The plan suited me perfectly, so we went up to the hospital, found Fargeau, who declared that he and Duchesne were ready for anything, the nearer the real "*bouche d'enfer*" the better; that the following Thursday they would both be off duty for the night, and that on that day they would join in an attempt to outwit the devil and clear up the mystery of No. 252.

"Does *M. l'Américain* go with us?" asked Fargeau.

"Why of course," I replied, "I intend to go, and you must not refuse me, d'Ardeche; I decline to be put off. Here is a chance for you to do the honours of your city in a manner which is faultless. Show me a real live ghost, and I will forgive Paris for having lost the Jardin Mabille."

So it was settled.

Later we went down to Meudon and ate dinner in the terrace room of the villa, which was all that d'Ardeche had said, and more, so utterly was its atmosphere that of the seventeenth century. At dinner Eugene told me more about his late aunt, and the queer goings on in the old house.

Mlle. Blaye lived, it seems, all alone, except for one female servant of her own age; a severe, taciturn creature, with massive Breton features and a Breton tongue, whenever she vouchsafed to use it. No one ever was seen to enter the door of No. 252 except Jeanne the servant and the Sar Torrevieja, the latter coming constantly from none knew whither, and always entering, *never leaving*. Indeed, the neighbours, who for eleven years had watched the old sorcerer sidle crab-wise up to the bell almost every day, declared vociferously that *never* had he been seen to leave the house. Once, when they decided to keep absolute guard, the watcher, none other than Maître Garceau of the Chien Bleu, after keeping his eyes fixed on the door from ten o'clock one morning when the *Sar* arrived until four in the afternoon, during which time the door was unopened (he knew this, for had he not gummed a ten-*centime* stamp over the joint and was not the stamp unbroken) nearly fell down when the sinister figure of Torrevieja slid wickedly by him with a dry "Pardon, *Monsieur!*" and disappeared again through the black doorway.

This was curious, for No. 252 was entirely surrounded by houses, its only windows opening on a courtyard into which no eye could look from the *hôtels* of the Rue M. le Prince and the Rue de l'Ecole, and the mystery was one of the choice possessions of the Latin Quarter.

Once a year the austerity of the place was broken, and the denizens of the whole quarter stood open-mouthed watching many carriages drive up to No. 252, many of them private, not a few with crests on the door panels, from all of them descending veiled female figures and men with coat collars turned up. Then followed curious sounds of music from within, and those whose houses joined the blank walls of No. 252 became for the moment popular, for by placing the ear against the wall strange music could distinctly be heard, and the sound of monotonous chanting voices now and then. By dawn the last guest would have departed, and for another year the *hôtel* of Mlle. de Tartas was ominously silent.

Eugene declared that he believed it was a celebration of "*Walpurgisnacht*," and certainly appearances favoured such a fancy.

"A queer thing about the whole affair is," he said, "the fact that everyone in the street swears that about a month ago, while I was out in Concarneau for a visit, the music and voices were heard again, just as when my revered aunt was in the flesh. The house was perfectly empty, as I tell you, so it is quite possible that the good people were enjoying an hallucination."

I must acknowledge that these stories did not reassure me; in fact, as Thursday came near, I began to regret a little my determination to spend the night in the house. I was too vain to back down, however, and the perfect coolness of the two doctors, who ran down Tuesday to Meudon to make a few arrangements, caused me to swear that I would die of fright before I would flinch. I suppose I believed more or less in ghosts, I am sure now that I am older I believe in them, there are in fact few things I can *not* believe. Two or three inexplicable things had happened to me, and, although this was before my adventure with Rendel in Pæstum, I had a strong predisposition to believe some things that I could not explain, wherein I was out of sympathy with the age.

Well, to come to the memorable night of the twelfth of June, we had made our preparations, and after depositing a big bag inside the doors of No. 252, went across to the Chien Bleu, where Fargeau and Duchesne turned up promptly, and we sat down to the best dinner Père Garceau could create.

I remember I hardly felt that the conversation was in good taste. It began with various stories of Indian *fakirs* and Oriental jugglery, matters in which Eugene was curiously well read, swerved to the horrors of the great *Sepoy* mutiny, and thus to reminiscences of the dissecting-room. By this time we had drunk more or less, and Duchesne launched into a photographic and Zolaesque account of the only time (as he said) when he was possessed of the panic of fear; namely, one night many years ago, when he was locked by accident into the dissecting-room of the Loucine, together with several cadavers of a rather unpleasant nature. I ventured to protest mildly against the choice of subjects, the result being a perfect carnival of horrors, so that when we finally drank our last *crème de cacao* and started for "*la Bouche d'Enfer*," my nerves were in a somewhat rocky condition.

It was just ten o'clock when we came into the street. A hot dead wind drifted in great puffs through the city, and ragged masses of vapour swept the purple sky; an unsavoury night altogether, one of those nights of hopeless lassitude when one feels, if one is at home, like doing nothing but drink mint juleps and smoke cigarettes.

Eugene opened the creaking door, and tried to light one of the lanterns; but the gusty wind blew out every match, and we finally had to close the outer doors before we could get a light. At last we had all the lanterns going, and I began to look around curiously. We were in a long, vaulted passage, partly carriageway, partly footpath, perfectly bare but for the street refuse which had drifted in with eddying winds. Beyond lay the courtyard, a curious place rendered more curious still by the fitful moonlight and the flashing of four dark lanterns. The place had evidently been once a most noble palace. Opposite rose the oldest portion, a three-story wall of the time of Francis I., with a great wisteria vine covering half. The wings on either side were more modern, seventeenth century, and ugly, while towards the street was nothing but a flat unbroken wall.

The great bare court, littered with bits of paper blown in by the wind, fragments of packing cases, and straw, mysterious with flashing lights and flaunting shadows, while low masses of torn vapour drifted overhead, hiding, then revealing the stars, and all in absolute silence, not even the sounds of the streets entering this prison-like place, was weird and uncanny in the extreme. I must confess that already I began to feel a slight disposition towards the horrors, but with that curious inconsequence which so often happens in the case of those who are deliberately growing scared, I could think of nothing more reassuring than those delicious verses of Lewis Carroll's:—

Just the place for a Snark! I have said it twice,
That alone should encourage the crew.
Just the place for a Snark! I have said it thrice,
What I tell you three times is true,—

which kept repeating themselves over and over in my brain with feverish insistence.

Even the medical students had stopped their chaffing, and were studying the surroundings gravely.

"There is one thing certain," said Fargeau, "*anything* might have happened here without the slightest chance of discovery. Did ever you see such a perfect place for lawlessness?"

"And *anything* might happen here now, with the same certainty of impunity," continued Duchesne, lighting his pipe, the snap of the match making us all start. "D'Ardeche, your lamented relative was certainly well fixed; she had full scope here for her traditional experiments in demonology."

"Curse me if I don't believe that those same traditions were more or less founded on fact," said Eugene. "I never saw this court under these conditions before, but I could believe anything now. What's that!"

"Nothing but a door slamming," said Duchesne, loudly.

"Well, I wish doors wouldn't slam in houses that have been empty eleven months."

"It is irritating," and Duchesne slipped his arm through mine; "but we must take things as they come. Remember we have to deal not only with the spectral lumber left here by your scarlet aunt, but as well with the supererogatory curse of that hell-cat Torrevieja. Come on! let's get inside before the hour arrives for the sheeted dead to squeak and gibber in these lonely halls. Light your pipes, your tobacco is a sure protection against 'your whoreson dead bodies'; light up and move on."

We opened the hall door and entered a vaulted stone vestibule, full of dust, and cobwebby.

"There is nothing on this floor," said Eugene, "except servants' rooms and offices, and I don't believe there is anything wrong with them. I never heard that there was, anyway. Let's go upstairs."

So far as we could see, the house was apparently perfectly uninteresting inside, all eighteenth-century work, the façade of the main building being, with the vestibule, the only portion of the Francis I. work.

"The place was burned during the Terror," said Eugene, "for my great-uncle, from whom Mlle. de Tartas inherited it, was a good and true Royalist; he went to Spain after the Revolution, and did not come back until the accession of Charles X., when he restored the house, and then died, enormously old. This explains why it is all so new."

The old Spanish sorcerer to whom Mlle. de Tartas had left her personal property had done his work thoroughly. The house was absolutely empty, even the wardrobes and bookcases built in had been carried away; we went through room after room, finding all absolutely dismantled, only the windows and doors with their casings, the parquet floors, and the florid Renaissance mantels remaining.

"I feel better," remarked Fargeau. "The house may be haunted, but it don't look it, certainly; it is the most respectable place imaginable."

"Just you wait," replied Eugene. "These are only the state apartments, which my aunt seldom used, except, perhaps, on her annual '*Walpurgisnacht.*' Come up stairs and I will show you a better *mise en scène.*"

On this floor, the rooms fronting the court, the sleeping-rooms, were quite small,—("They are the bad rooms all the same," said Eugene,)—four of them, all just as ordinary in appearance as those below. A corridor ran behind them connecting with the wing corridor, and from this opened a door, unlike any of the other doors in that it was covered with green baize, somewhat moth-eaten. Eugene selected a key from the bunch he carried, unlocked the door, and with some difficulty forced it to swing inward; it was as heavy as the door of a safe.

"We are now," he said, "on the very threshold of hell itself; these rooms in here were my scarlet aunt's unholy of unholies. I never let them with the rest of the house, but keep them as a curiosity. I only wish Torrevieja had kept out; as it was, he looted them, as he did the rest of the house, and nothing is left but the walls and ceiling and floor. They are something, however, and may suggest what the former condition must have been. Tremble and enter."

The first apartment was a kind of anteroom, a cube of perhaps twenty feet each way, without windows, and with no doors except that by which we entered and another to the right. Walls, floor, and ceiling were covered with a black lacquer, brilliantly polished, that flashed the light of our lanterns in a thousand intricate reflections. It was like the inside of an enormous Japanese box, and about as empty. From this we passed to another room, and here we nearly dropped our lanterns.

The room was circular, thirty feet or so in diameter, covered by a hemispherical dome; walls and ceiling were dark blue, spotted with gold stars; and reaching from floor to floor across the dome stretched a colossal figure in red lacquer of a nude woman kneeling, her legs reaching out along the floor on either side, her head touching the lintel of the door through which we had entered, her arms forming its sides, with the fore arms extended and stretching along the walls until they met the long feet. The most astounding, misshapen, absolutely terrifying thing, I think, I ever saw. From the navel hung a great white object, like the traditional roe's egg of the *Arabian Nights*. The floor was of red lacquer, and in it was inlaid a pentagram the size of the room, made of wide strips of brass. In the centre of this pentagram was a circular disk of black stone, slightly saucer-shaped, with a small outlet in the middle.

The effect of the room was simply crushing, with this gigantic red figure crouched over it all, the staring eyes fixed on one, no matter what his position. None of us spoke, so oppressive was the whole thing.

The third room was like the first in dimensions, but instead of being black it was entirely sheathed with plates of brass, walls, ceiling, and floor,—tarnished now, and turning green, but still brilliant under the lantern light. In the middle stood an oblong altar of porphyry, its longer dimensions on the axis of the suite of rooms, and at one end, opposite the range of doors, a pedestal of black basalt.

This was all. Three rooms, stranger than these, even in their emptiness, it would be hard to imagine. In Egypt, in India, they would not be entirely out of place, but here in Paris, in a commonplace *hôtel*, in the Rue M. le Prince, they were incredible.

We retraced our steps, Eugene closed the iron door with its baize covering, and we went into one of the front chambers and sat down, looking at each other.

"Nice party, your aunt," said Fargeau. "Nice old party, with amiable tastes; I am glad we are not to spend the night in *those* rooms."

"What do you suppose she did there?" inquired Duchesne. "I know more or less about black art, but that series of rooms is too much for me."

"My impression is," said d'Ardeche, "that the brazen room was a kind of sanctuary containing some image or other on the basalt base, while the stone in front was really an altar,—

what the nature of the sacrifice might be I don't even guess. The round room may have been used for invocations and incantations. The pentagram looks like it. Any way it is all just about as queer and *fin de siècle* as I can well imagine. Look here, it is nearly twelve, let's dispose of ourselves, if we are going to hunt this thing down."

The four chambers on this floor of the old house were those said to be haunted, the wings being quite innocent, and, so far as we knew, the floors below. It was arranged that we should each occupy a room, leaving the doors open with the lights burning, and at the slightest cry or knock we were all to rush at once to the room from which the warning sound might come. There was no communication between the rooms to be sure, but, as the doors all opened into the corridor, every sound was plainly audible.

The last room fell to me, and I looked it over carefully.

It seemed innocent enough, a commonplace, square, rather lofty Parisian sleeping-room, finished in wood painted white, with a small marble mantel, a dusty floor of inlaid maple and cherry, walls hung with an ordinary French paper, apparently quite new, and two deeply embrasured windows looking out on the court.

I opened the swinging sash with some trouble, and sat down in the window seat with my lantern beside me trained on the only door, which gave on the corridor.

The wind had gone down, and it was very still without,—still and hot. The masses of luminous vapour were gathering thickly overhead, no longer urged by the gusty wind. The great masses of rank wisteria leaves, with here and there a second blossoming of purple flowers, hung dead over the window in the sluggish air. Across the roofs I could hear the sound of a belated *fiacre* in the streets below. I filled my pipe again and waited.

For a time the voices of the men in the other rooms were a companionship, and at first I shouted to them now and then, but my voice echoed rather unpleasantly through the long corridors, and had a suggestive way of reverberating around the left wing beside me, and coming out at a broken window at its extremity like the voice of another man. I soon gave up my attempts at conversation, and devoted myself to the task of keeping awake.

It was not easy; why did I eat that lettuce salad at Père Garceau's? I should have known better. It was making me irresistibly sleepy, and wakefulness was absolutely necessary. It was certainly gratifying to know that I could sleep, that my courage was by me to that extent, but in the interests of science I must keep awake. But almost never, it seemed, had sleep looked so desirable. Half a hundred times, nearly, I would doze for an instant, only to awake with a start, and find my pipe gone out. Nor did the exertion of relighting it pull me together.

I struck my match mechanically, and with the first puff dropped off again. It was most vexing. I got up and walked around the room. It was most annoying. My cramped position had almost put both my legs to sleep. I could hardly stand. I felt numb, as though with cold. There was no longer any sound from the other rooms, nor from without. I sank down in my window seat. How dark it was growing! I turned up the lantern. That pipe again, how obstinately it kept going out! and my last match was gone. The lantern, too, was *that* going out? I lifted my hand to turn it up again. It felt like lead, and fell beside me.

Then I awoke,—absolutely. I remembered the story of *The Haunters and the Haunted. This* was the Horror. I tried to rise, to cry out. My body was like lead, my tongue was paralyzed. I could hardly move my eyes. And the light was going out. There was no question about that. Darker and darker yet; little by little the pattern of the paper was swallowed up in the advancing night. A prickling numbness gathered in every nerve, my right arm slipped without feeling from my lap to my side, and I could not raise it,—it swung helpless. A thin, keen humming began in my head, like the cicadas on a hillside in September. The darkness was coming fast.

Yes, this was it. Something was subjecting me, body and mind, to slow paralysis. Physically I was already dead. If I could only hold my mind, my consciousness, I might still be safe, but could

I? Could I resist the mad horror of this silence, the deepening dark, the creeping numbness? I knew that, like the man in the ghost story, my only safety lay here.

It had come at last. My body was dead, I could no longer move my eyes. They were fixed in that last look on the place where the door had been, now only a deepening of the dark.

Utter night: the last flicker of the lantern was gone. I sat and waited; my mind was still keen, but how long would it last? There was a limit even to the endurance of the utter panic of fear.

Then the end began. In the velvet blackness came two white eyes, milky, opalescent, small, far away,—awful eyes, like a dead dream. More beautiful than I can describe, the flakes of white flame moving from the perimeter inward, disappearing in the centre, like a never ending flow of opal water into a circular tunnel. I could not have moved my eyes had I possessed the power: they devoured the fearful, beautiful things that grew slowly, slowly larger, fixed on me, advancing, growing more beautiful, the white flakes of light sweeping more swiftly into the blazing vortices, the awful fascination deepening in its insane intensity as the white, vibrating eyes grew nearer, larger.

Like a hideous and implacable engine of death the eyes of the unknown Horror swelled and expanded until they were close before me, enormous, terrible, and I felt a slow, cold, wet breath propelled with mechanical regularity against my face, enveloping me in its fetid mist, in its charnel-house deadliness.

With ordinary fear goes always a physical terror, but with me in the presence of this unspeakable Thing was only the utter and awful terror of the mind, the mad fear of a prolonged and ghostly nightmare. Again and again I tried to shriek, to make some noise, but physically I was utterly dead. I could only feel myself go mad with the terror of hideous death. The eyes were close on me,—their movement so swift that they seemed to be but palpitating flames, the dead breath was around me like the depths of the deepest sea.

Suddenly a wet, icy mouth, like that of a dead cuttle-fish,

shapeless, jelly-like, fell over mine. The horror began slowly to draw my life from me, but, as enormous and shuddering folds of palpitating jelly swept sinuously around me, my will came back, my body awoke with the reaction of final fear, and I closed with the nameless death that enfolded me.

What was it that I was fighting? My arms sunk through the unresisting mass that was turning me to ice. Moment by moment new folds of cold jelly swept round me, crushing me with the force of Titans. I fought to wrest my mouth from this awful Thing that sealed it, but, if ever I succeeded and caught a single breath, the wet, sucking mass closed over my face again before I could cry out. I think I fought for hours, desperately, insanely, in a silence that was more hideous than any sound,—fought until I felt final death at hand, until the memory of all my life rushed over me like a flood, until I no longer had strength to wrench my face from that hellish succubus, until with a last mechanical struggle I fell and yielded to death.

★   ★   ★   ★   ★

Then I heard a voice say, "If he is dead, I can never forgive myself; I was to blame."

Another replied, "He is not dead, I know we can save him if only we reach the hospital in time. Drive like hell, *cocher*! twenty *francs* for you, if you get there in three minutes."

Then there was night again, and nothingness, until I suddenly awoke and stared around. I lay in a hospital ward, very white and sunny, some yellow *fleurs-de-lis* stood beside the head of the pallet, and a tall sister of mercy sat by my side.

To tell the story in a few words, I was in the Hôtel Dieu, where the men had taken me that fearful night of the twelfth of June. I asked for Fargeau or Duchesne, and by and by the latter came, and sitting beside the bed told me all that I did not know.

It seems that they had sat, each in his room, hour after hour, hearing nothing, very much bored, and disappointed. Soon after two o'clock Fargeau, who was in the next room, called to me to ask if I was awake. I gave no reply, and, after shouting once or twice, he took his lantern and came to investigate. The door was locked on the inside! He instantly called d'Ardeche and Duchesne, and together they hurled themselves against the door. It resisted. Within they could hear irregular footsteps dashing here and there, with heavy breathing. Although frozen with terror, they fought to destroy the door and finally succeeded by using a great slab of marble that formed the shelf of the mantel in Fargeau's room. As the door crashed in, they were suddenly hurled back against the walls of the corridor, as though by an explosion, the lanterns were extinguished, and they found themselves in utter silence and darkness.

As soon as they recovered from the shock, they leaped into the room and fell over my body in the middle of the floor. They lighted one of the lanterns, and saw the strangest sight that can be imagined. The floor and walls to the height of about six feet were running with something that seemed like stagnant water, thick, glutinous, sickening. As for me, I was drenched with the same cursed liquid. The odour of musk was nauseating. They dragged me away, stripped off my clothing, wrapped me in their coats, and hurried to the hospital, thinking me perhaps dead.

Soon after sunrise d'Ardeche left the hospital, being assured that I was in a fair way to recovery, with time, and with Fargeau went up to examine by daylight the traces of the adventure that was so nearly fatal. They were too late. Fire engines were coming down the street as they passed the Académie. A neighbor rushed up to d'Ardeche: "O *Monsieur*! what misfortune, yet what fortune! It is true *la Bouche d'Enfer*—I beg pardon, the residence of the lamented Mlle. de Tartas,—was burned, but not wholly, only the ancient building. The wings were saved, and for that great credit is due the brave firemen. *Monsieur* will remember them, no doubt."

It was quite true. Whether a forgotten lantern, overturned in the excitement, had done the work, or whether the origin of the fire was more supernatural, it was certain that "the Mouth of Hell" was no more. A last engine was pumping slowly as d'Ardeche came up; half a dozen limp, and one distended, hose stretched through the *porte cochère*, and within only the façade of Francis I. remained, draped still with the black stems of the wisteria. Beyond lay a great vacancy, where thin smoke was rising slowly. Every floor was gone, and the strange halls of Mlle. Blaye de Tartas were only a memory.

With d'Ardeche I visited the place last year, but in the stead of the ancient walls was then only a new and ordinary building, fresh and respectable; yet the wonderful stories of the old *Bouche d'Enfer* still lingered in the quarter, and will hold there, I do not doubt, until the Day of Judgement.

In Kropfsberg Keep

To the traveller from Innsbrück to Munich, up the lovely valley of the silver Inn, many castles appear, one after another, each on its beetling cliff or gentle hill,—appear and disappear, melting into the dark fir trees that grow so thickly on every side,—Laneck, Lichtwer, Ratholtz, Tratzberg, Matzen, Kropfsberg, gathering close around the entrance to the dark and wonderful Zillerthal.

But to us—Tom Rendel and myself—there are two castles only: not the gorgeous and princely Ambras, nor the noble old Tratzberg, with its crowded treasures of solemn and splendid medievalism; but little Matzen, where eager hospitality forms the new life of a never-dead chivalry, and Kropfsberg, ruined, tottering, blasted by fire and smitten with grievous years,—a dead thing, and haunted,—full of strange legends, and eloquent of mystery and tragedy.

We were visiting the von C——s at Matzen, and gaining our first wondering knowledge of the courtly, cordial castle life in the Tyrol,—of the gentle and delicate hospitality of noble Austrians. Brixleg had ceased to be but a mark on a map, and had become a place of rest and delight, a home for homeless wanderers on the face of Europe, while Schloss Matzen was a synonym for all that was gracious and kindly and beautiful in life. The days moved on in a golden round of riding and driving and shooting: down to Landl and Thiersee for chamois, across the river to the magic Achensee, up the Zillerthal, across the Schmerner Joch, even to the railway station at Steinach.

And in the evenings after the late dinners in the upper hall where the sleepy hounds leaned against our chairs looking at us with suppliant eyes, in the evenings when the fire was dying away in the hooded fireplace in the library, stories. Stories, and legends, and fairy tales, while the stiff old portraits changed countenance constantly under the flickering firelight, and the sound of the drifting Inn came softly across the meadows far below.

If ever I tell the *Story of Schloss Matzen,* then will be the time to paint the too inadequate picture of this fair oasis in the desert of travel and tourists and hotels; but just now it is Kropfsberg the Silent that is of greater importance, for it was only in Matzen that the story was told by Fräulein E——, the gold-haired niece of Frau von C——, one hot evening in July, when we were sitting in the great west window of the drawing-room after a long ride up the Stallenthal. All the windows were open to catch the faint wind, and we had sat for a long time watching the Otzethaler Alps turn rose-colour over distant Innsbrück, then deepen to violet as the sun went down and the white mists rose slowly until Lichtwer and Laneck and Kropfsberg rose like craggy islands in a silver sea.

And this is the story as Fräulein E—— told it to us,—the Story of Kropfsberg Keep.

★ ★ ★ ★ ★

A great many years ago, soon after my grandfather died, and Matzen came to us, when I was a little girl, and so young that I remember nothing of the affair except as something dreadful that frightened me very much, two young men who had studied painting with my grandfather came down to Brixleg from Munich, partly to paint, and partly to amuse themselves,—"ghost-hunting" as they said, for they were very sensible young men and prided themselves on it, laughing at all kinds of "superstition," and particularly at that form which believed in ghosts and feared them. They had never seen a real ghost, you know, and they belonged to a certain set of people who believed nothing they had not seen themselves,—which always seemed to me *very* conceited. Well, they knew that we had lots of beautiful castles here in the "lower valley," and they assumed, and rightly, that every castle has at least *one* ghost story connected with it, so they chose this as their hunting ground, only the game they sought was ghosts, not chamois. Their plan was to visit every place that was supposed to be haunted, and to meet every reputed ghost, and prove that it really was no ghost at all.

There was a little inn down in the village then, kept by an old man named Peter Rosskopf, and the two young men made this their headquarters. The very first night they began to draw from the old innkeeper all that he knew of legends and ghost stories connected with Brixleg and its castles, and as he was a most garrulous old gentleman he filled them with the wildest delight by his stories of the ghosts of the castles about the mouth of the Zillerthal.

Of course the old man believed every word he said, and you can imagine his horror and amazement when, after telling his guests the particularly blood-curdling story of Kropfsberg and its haunted keep, the elder of the two boys, whose surname I have forgotten, but whose Christian name was Rupert, calmly said, "Your story is most satisfactory: we will sleep in Kropfsberg Keep tomorrow night, and you must provide us with all that we may need to make ourselves comfortable."

The old man nearly fell into the fire. "What for a block-head are you?" he cried, with big eyes. "The keep is haunted by Count Albert's ghost, I tell you!"

"That is why we are going there tomorrow night; we wish to make the acquaintance of Count Albert."

"But there was a man stayed there once, and in the morning he was dead."

"Very silly of him; there are two of us, and we carry revolvers."

"But it's a *ghost*, I tell you," almost screamed the innkeeper; "are ghosts afraid of firearms?"

"Whether they are or not, we are *not* afraid of *them*."

149

Here the younger boy broke in,—he was named Otto von Kleist. I remember the name, for I had a music teacher once by that name. He abused the poor old man shamefully; told him that they were going to spend the night in Kropfsberg in spite of Count Albert and Peter Rosskopf, and that he might as well make the most of it and earn his money with cheerfulness.

In a word, they finally bullied the old fellow into submission, and when the morning came he set about preparing for the suicide, as he considered it, with sighs and mutterings and ominous shakings of the head.

You know the condition of the castle now,—nothing but scorched walls and crumbling piles of fallen masonry. Well, at the time I tell you of, the keep was still partially preserved. It was finally burned out only a few years ago by some wicked boys who came over from Jenbach to have a good time. But when the ghost hunters came, though the two lower floors had fallen into the crypt, the third floor remained. The peasants said it *could* not fall, but that it would stay until the Day of Judgment, because it was in the room above that the wicked Count Albert sat watching the flames destroy the great castle and his imprisoned guests, and where he finally hung himself in a suit of armour that had belonged to his medieval ancestor, the first Count Kropfsberg.

No one dared touch him, and so he hung there for twelve years, and all the time venturesome boys and daring men used to creep up the turret steps and stare awfully through the chinks in the door at that ghostly mass of steel that held within itself the body of a murderer and suicide, slowly returning to the dust from which it was made. Finally it disappeared, none knew whither, and for another dozen years the room stood empty but for the old furniture and the rotting hangings.

So, when the two men climbed the stairway to the haunted room, they found a very different state of things from what exists now. The room was absolutely as it was left the night Count Albert burned the castle, except that all trace of the suspended suit of armour and its ghastly contents had vanished.

No one had dared to cross the threshold, and I suppose that

for forty years no living thing had entered that dreadful room.

On one side stood a vast canopied bed of black wood, the damask hangings of which were covered with mould and mildew. All the clothing of the bed was in perfect order, and on it lay a book, open, and face downward. The only other furniture in the room consisted of several old chairs, a carved oak chest, and a big inlaid table covered with books and papers, and on one corner two or three bottles with dark solid sediment at the bottom, and a glass, also dark with the dregs of wine that had been poured out almost half a century before. The tapestry on the walls was green with mould, but hardly torn or otherwise defaced, for although the heavy dust of forty years lay on everything the room had been preserved from further harm. No spider web was to be seen, no trace of nibbling mice, not even a dead moth or fly on the sills of the diamond-paned windows; life seemed to have shunned the room utterly and finally.

The men looked at the room curiously, and, I am sure, not without some feelings of awe and unacknowledged fear; but, whatever they may have felt of instinctive shrinking, they said nothing, and quickly set to work to make the room passably inhabitable. They decided to touch nothing that had not absolutely to be changed, and therefore they made for themselves a bed in one corner with the mattress and linen from the inn. In the great fireplace they piled a lot of wood on the caked ashes of a fire dead for forty years, turned the old chest into a table, and laid out on it all their arrangements for the evening's amusement: food, two or three bottles of wine, pipes and tobacco, and the chess-board that was their inseparable travelling companion.

All this they did themselves: the innkeeper would not even come within the walls of the outer court; he insisted that he had washed his hands of the whole affair, the silly dunderheads might go to their death their own way. *He* would not aid and abet them. One of the stable boys brought the basket of food and the wood and the bed up the winding stone stairs, to be sure, but neither money nor prayers nor threats would bring him within the walls of the accursed place, and he stared fearfully at the hare-brained boys as they worked around the dead old room preparing for the night that was coming so fast.

At length everything was in readiness, and after a final visit to the inn for dinner Rupert and Otto started at sunset for the Keep. Half the village went with them, for Peter Rosskopf had babbled the whole story to an open-mouthed crowd of wondering men and women, and as to an execution the awe-struck crowd followed the two boys dumbly, curious to see if they surely would put their plan into execution. But none went farther than the outer doorway of the stairs, for it was already growing twilight. In absolute silence they watched the two fool-hardy youths with their lives in their hands enter the terrible Keep, standing like a tower in the midst of the piles of stones that had once formed walls joining it with the mass of the castle beyond. When a moment later a light showed itself in the high windows above, they sighed resignedly and went their ways, to wait stolidly until morning should come and prove the truth of their fears and warnings.

In the meantime the ghost hunters built a huge fire, lighted their many candles, and sat down to await developments. Rupert afterwards told my uncle that they really felt no fear whatever, only a contemptuous curiosity, and they ate their supper with good appetite and an unusual relish. It was a long evening. They played many games of chess, waiting for midnight. Hour passed after hour, and nothing occurred to interrupt the monotony of the evening. Ten, eleven, came and went,—it was almost midnight. They piled more wood in the fireplace, lighted new candles, looked to their pistols—and waited. The clocks in the village struck twelve; the sound coming muffled through the high, deep-embrasured windows. Nothing happened, nothing to break the heavy silence; and with a feeling of disappointed relief they looked at each other and acknowledged that they had met another rebuff.

Finally they decided that there was no use in sitting up and boring themselves any longer, they had much better rest; so Otto threw himself down on the mattress, falling almost immediately asleep. Rupert sat a little longer, smoking, and watching the stars creep along behind the shattered glass and the bent leads of the lofty windows; watching the fire fall together, and the strange shadows move mysteriously on the mouldering walls. The iron hook in the oak beam, that crossed the ceiling midway, fascinated him, not with fear, but morbidly.

So, it was from that hook that for twelve years, twelve long years of changing summer and winter, the body of Count Albert, murderer and suicide, hung in its strange casing of medieval steel; moving a little at first, and turning gently while the fire died out on the hearth, while the ruins of the castle grew cold, and horrified peasants sought for the bodies of the score of gay, reckless, wicked guests whom Count Albert had gathered in Kropfsberg for a last debauch, gathered to their terrible and untimely death.

What a strange and fiendish idea it was, the young, handsome noble who had ruined himself and his family in the society of the splendid debauchees, gathering them all together, men and women who had known only love and pleasure, for a glorious and awful riot of luxury, and then, when they were all dancing in the great ballroom, locking the doors and burning the whole castle about them, the while he sat in the great keep listening to their screams of agonized fear, watching the fire sweep from wing to wing until the whole mighty mass was one enormous and awful pyre, and then, clothing himself in his great-great-grandfather's armour, hanging himself in the midst of the ruins of what had been a proud and noble castle. So ended a great family, a great house.

But that was forty years ago.

He was growing drowsy; the light flickered and flared in the fireplace; one by one the candles went out; the shadows grew thick in the room. Why did that great iron hook stand out so plainly? why did that dark shadow dance and quiver so mockingly behind it?—why—But he ceased to wonder at anything. He was asleep.

It seemed to him that he woke almost immediately; the fire

still burned, though low and fitfully on the hearth. Otto was sleeping, breathing quietly and regularly; the shadows had gathered close around him, thick and murky; with every passing moment the light died in the fireplace; he felt stiff with cold. In the utter silence he heard the clock in the village strike two. He shivered with a sudden and irresistible feeling of fear, and abruptly turned and looked towards the hook in the ceiling.

Yes, It was there. He knew that It would be. It seemed quite natural, he would have been disappointed had he seen nothing; but now he knew that the story was true, knew that he was wrong, and that the dead *do* sometimes return to earth, for there, in the fast-deepening shadow, hung the black mass of wrought steel, turning a little now and then, with the light flickering on the tarnished and rusty metal. He watched it quietly; he hardly felt afraid; it was rather a sentiment of sadness and fatality that filled him, of gloomy forebodings of something unknown, unimaginable. He sat and watched the thing disappear in the gathering dark, his hand on his pistol as it lay by him on the great chest. There was no sound but the regular breathing of the sleeping boy on the mattress.

It had grown absolutely dark; a bat fluttered against the broken glass of the window. He wondered if he was growing mad, for—he hesitated to acknowledge it to himself—he heard music; far, curious music, a strange and luxurious dance, very faint, very vague, but unmistakable.

Like a flash of lightning came a jagged line of fire down the blank wall opposite him, a line that remained, that grew wider, that let a pale cold light into the room, showing him now all its details,—the empty fireplace, where a thin smoke rose in a spiral from a bit of charred wood, the mass of the great bed, and, in the very middle, black against the curious brightness, the armoured man, or ghost, or devil, standing, not suspended, beneath the rusty hook. And with the rending of the wall the music grew more distinct, though sounding still very, very far away.

Count Albert raised his mailed hand and beckoned to him; then turned, and stood in the riven wall.

Without a word, Rupert rose and followed him, his pistol in hand. Count Albert passed through the mighty wall and disappeared in the unearthly light. Rupert followed mechanically. He felt the crushing of the mortar beneath his feet, the roughness of the jagged wall where he rested his hand to steady himself.

The keep rose absolutely isolated among the ruins, yet on passing through the wall Rupert found himself in a long, uneven corridor, the floor of which was warped and sagging, while the walls were covered on one side with big faded portraits of an inferior quality, like those in the corridor that connects the Pitti and Uffizzi in Florence. Before him moved the figure of Count Albert,—a black silhouette in the ever-increasing light. And always the music grew stronger and stranger, a mad, evil, seductive dance that bewitched even while it disgusted.

In a final blaze of vivid, intolerable light, in a burst of hellish music that might have come from Bedlam, Rupert stepped from the corridor into a vast and curious room where at first he saw nothing, distinguished nothing but a mad, seething whirl of sweeping figures, white, in a white room, under white light, Count Albert standing before him, the only dark object to be seen. As his eyes grew accustomed to the fearful brightness, he knew that he was looking on a dance such as the damned might see in hell, but such as no living man had ever seen before.

Around the long, narrow hall, under the fearful light that came from nowhere, but was omnipresent, swept a rushing stream of unspeakable horrors, dancing insanely, laughing, gibbering hideously; the dead of forty years. White, polished skeletons, bare of flesh and vesture, skeletons clothed in the dreadful rags of dried and rattling sinews, the tags of tattering grave-clothes flaunting behind them. These were the dead of many years ago. Then the dead of more recent times, with yellow bones showing only here and there, the long and insecure hair of their hideous heads writhing in the beating air. Then green and gray horrors, bloated and shapeless, stained with earth or dripping with spattering water; and here and there white, beautiful things, like chiselled ivory, the dead of yesterday, locked it may be, in the mummy arms of rattling skeletons.

Round and round the cursed room, a swaying, swirling maelstrom of death, while the air grew thick with miasma, the floor foul with shreds of shrouds, and yellow parchment, clattering bones, and wisps of tangled hair.

And in the very midst of this ring of death, a sight not for words nor for thought, a sight to blast forever the mind of the man who looked upon it: a leaping, writhing dance of Count Albert's victims, the score of beautiful women and reckless men who danced to their awful death while the castle burned around them, charred and shapeless now, a living charnel-house of nameless horror.

Count Albert, who had stood silent and gloomy, watching the dance of the damned, turned to Rupert, and for the first time spoke.

"We are ready for you now; dance!"

A prancing horror, dead some dozen years, perhaps, flaunted from the rushing river of the dead, and leered at Rupert with eyeless skull.

"Dance!"

Rupert stood frozen, motionless.

"Dance!"

His hard lips moved. "Not if the devil came from hell to make me."

Count Albert swept his vast two-handed sword into the foetid air while the tide of corruption paused in its swirling, and swept down on Rupert with gibbering grins.

The room, and the howling dead, and the black portent before him circled dizzily around, as with a last effort of departing consciousness he drew his pistol and fired full in the face of Count Albert.

★   ★   ★   ★   ★

Perfect silence, perfect darkness; not a breath, not a sound: the dead stillness of a long-sealed tomb. Rupert lay on his back, stunned, helpless, his pistol clenched in his frozen hand, a smell of powder in the black air. Where was he? Dead? In hell? He reached his hand out cautiously; it fell on dusty boards. Outside, far away, a clock struck three. Had he dreamed? Of course; but how ghastly a dream! With chattering teeth he called softly,—

"Otto!"

There was no reply, and none when he called again and again. He staggered weakly to his feet, groping for matches and candles. A panic of abject terror came on him; the matches were gone! He turned towards the fireplace: a single coal glowed in the white ashes. He swept a mass of papers and dusty books from the table, and with trembling hands cowered over the embers, until he succeeded in lighting the dry tinder. Then he piled the old books on the blaze, and looked fearfully around.

No: It was gone,—thank God for that; the hook was empty.

But why did Otto sleep so soundly; why did he not awake?

He stepped unsteadily across the room in the flaring light of the burning books, and knelt by the mattress.

★　★　★　★　★

So they found him in the morning, when no one came to the inn from Kropfsberg Keep, and the quaking Peter Rosskopf arranged a relief party;—found him kneeling beside the mattress where Otto lay, shot in the throat and quite dead.

The White Villa

When we left Naples on the 8.10 train for Pæstum, Tom and I, we fully intended returning by the 2.46. Not because two hours time seemed enough wherein to exhaust the interests of those deathless ruins of a dead civilization, but simply for the reason that, as our *Indicatore* informed us, there was but one other train, and that at 6.11, which would land us in Naples too late for the dinner at the Turners and the San Carlo afterwards. Not that I cared in the least for the dinner or the theatre; but then, I was not so obviously in Miss Turner's good graces as Tom Rendel was, which made a difference.

However, we had promised, so that was an end of it.

This was in the spring of '88, and at that time the railroad, which was being pushed onward to Reggio, whereby travellers to Sicily might be spared the agonies of a night on the fickle Mediterranean, reached no farther than Agropoli, some twenty miles beyond Pæstum; but although the trains were as yet few and slow, we accepted the half-finished road with gratitude, for it penetrated the very centre of Campanian brigandage, and made it possible for us to see the matchless temples in safety, while a few years before it was necessary for intending visitors to obtain a military escort from the Government; and military escorts are not for young architects.

So we set off contentedly, that white May morning, determined to make the best of our few hours, little thinking that before we saw Naples again we were to witness things that perhaps no American had ever seen before.

For a moment, when we left the train at "Pesto," and started to walk up the flowery lane leading to the temples, we were almost inclined to curse this same railroad. We had thought, in our innocence, that we should be alone, that no one else would think of enduring the long four hours' ride from Naples just to spend two hours in the ruins of these temples; but the event proved our unwisdom. We were *not* alone. It was a compact little party of conventional sightseers that accompanied us. The inevitable English family with the three daughters, prominent of teeth, flowing of hair, aggressive of scarlet Murrays and Baedekers; the two blond and untidy Germans; a French couple from the pages of *La Vie Parisienne*; and our "old man of the sea," the white-bearded Presbyterian minister from Pennsylvania who had made our life miserable in Rome at the time of the Pope's Jubilee. Fortunately for us, this terrible old man had fastened himself upon a party of American schoolteachers travelling *en Cook*, and for the time we were safe; but our vision of two hours of dreamy solitude faded lamentably away.

Yet how beautiful it was! this golden meadow walled with far, violet mountains, breathless under a May sun; and in the midst, rising from tangles of asphodel and acanthus, vast in the vacant plain, three temples, one silver gray, one golden gray, and one flushed with intangible rose. And all around nothing but velvet meadows stretching from the dim mountains behind, away to the sea, that showed only as a thin line of silver just over the edge of the still grass.

The tide of tourists swept noisily through the Basilica and the temple of Poseidon across the meadow to the distant temple of Ceres, and Tom and I were left alone to drink in all the fine wine of dreams that was possible in the time left us. We gave but little space to examining the temples the tourists had left, but in a few moments found ourselves lying in the grass to the east of Poseidon, looking dimly out towards the sea, heard now, but not seen,—a vague and pulsating murmur that blended with the humming of bees all about us.

A small shepherd boy, with a woolly dog, made shy advances

of friendship, and in a little time we had set him to gathering flowers for us: asphodels and bee-orchids, anemones, and the little thin green iris so fairylike and frail. The murmur of the tourist crowd had merged itself in the moan of the sea, and it was very still; suddenly I heard the words I had been waiting for,—the suggestion I had refrained from making myself, for I knew Thomas.

"I say, old man, shall we let the 2.46 go to thunder?"

I chuckled to myself. "But the Turners?"

"They be blowed, we can tell them we missed the train."

"That is just exactly what we shall do," I said, pulling out my watch, "unless we start for the station right now."

But Tom drew an acanthus leaf across his face and showed no signs of moving; so I filled my pipe again, and we missed the train.

As the sun dropped lower towards the sea, changing its silver line to gold, we pulled ourselves together, and for an hour or more sketched vigorously; but the mood was not on us. It was "too jolly fine to waste time working," as Tom said; so we started off to explore the single street of the squalid town of Pesto that was lost within the walls of dead Poseidonia. It was not a pretty village,—if you can call a rut-riven lane and a dozen houses a village,—nor were the inhabitants thereof reassuring in appearance. There was no sign of a church,—nothing but dirty huts, and in the midst, one of two stories, rejoicing in the name of *Albergo del Sole*, the first story of which was a black and cavernous smithy, where certain swarthy knaves, looking like *banditti* out of a job, sat smoking sulkily.

"We might stay here all night," said Tom, grinning askance at this choice company; but his suggestion was not received with enthusiasm.

Down where the lane from the station joined the main road stood the only sign of modern civilization,—a great square structure, half villa, half fortress, with round turrets on its four corners, and a ten-foot wall surrounding it. There were no windows in its first story, so far as we could see, and it had evidently been at one time the fortified villa of some Campanian noble. Now, however, whether because brigandage had been stamped out, or because the villa was empty and deserted, it was no longer formidable; the gates of the great wall hung sagging on their hinges, brambles growing all over them, and many of the windows in the upper story were broken and black. It was a strange place, weird and mysterious, and we looked at it curiously. "There is a story about that place," said Tom, with conviction.

It was growing late: the sun was near the edge of the sea as we walked down the ivy-grown walls of the vanished city for the last time, and as we turned back, a red flush poured from the west, and painted the Doric temples in pallid rose against the evanescent purple of the Apennines. Already a thin mist was rising from the meadows, and the temples hung pink in the misty grayness.

It was a sorrow to leave the beautiful things, but we could run no risk of missing this last train, so we walked slowly back towards the temples.

"What is that Johnny waving his arm at us for?" asked Tom, suddenly.

"How should I know? We are not on his land, and the walls don't matter."

We pulled out our watches simultaneously.

"What time are you?" I said.

"Six minutes before six."

"And I am seven minutes. It can't take us all that time to walk to the station."

"Are you sure the train goes at 6.11?"

"Dead sure," I answered; and showed him the *Indicatore*.

By this time a woman and two children were shrieking at us hysterically; but what they said I had no idea, their Italian being of a strange and awful nature.

"Look here," I said, "let's run; perhaps our watches are both slow."

"Or—perhaps the time-table is changed."

Then we ran, and the populace cheered and shouted with

enthusiasm; our dignified run became a panic-stricken rout, for as we turned into the lane, smoke was rising from beyond the bank that hid the railroad; a bell rang; we were so near that we could hear the interrogative *Pronte?* the impatient *Partenza!* and the definitive *Andiamo!* But the train was five hundred yards away, steaming towards Naples, when we plunged into the station as the clock struck six, and yelled for the station-master.

He came, and we indulged in crimination and recrimination.

When we could regard the situation calmly, it became apparent that the time-table *had* been changed two days before, the 6.11 now leaving at 5.58. A *facchino* came in, and we four sat down and regarded the situation judicially.

"Was there any other train?"

"No."

"Could we stay at the Albergo del Sole?"

A forefinger drawn across the throat by the Capo Stazione with a significant "cluck" closed that question.

"Then we must stay with you here at the station."

"But, *Signori*, I am not married. I live here only with the *facchini*. I have only one room to sleep in. It is impossible!"

"But we must sleep somewhere, likewise eat. What can we do?" and we shifted the responsibility deftly on the shoulders of the poor old man, who was growing excited again.

He trotted nervously up and down the station for a minute, then he called the *facchino*. "Giuseppe, go up to the villa and ask if two *forestieri* who have missed the last train can stay there all night!"

Protests were useless. The *facchino* was gone, and we waited anxiously for his return. It seemed as though he would never come. Darkness had fallen, and the moon was rising over the mountains. At last he appeared.

"The *Signori* may stay all night, and welcome; but they cannot come to dinner, for there is nothing in the house to eat!"

This was not reassuring, and again the old station-master lost himself in meditation. The results were admirable, for in a little time the table in the waiting-room had been transformed into a dining-table, and Tom and I were ravenously devouring a big omelette, and bread and cheese, and drinking a most shocking sour wine as though it were Château Yquem. A *facchino* served us, with clumsy goodwill; and when we had induced our nervous old host to sit down with us and partake of his own hospitality, we succeeded in forming a passably jolly dinner-party, forgetting over our sour wine and cigarettes the coming hours from ten until sunrise, which lay before us in a dubious mist.

It was with crowding apprehensions which we strove in vain to joke away that we set out at last to retrace our steps to the mysterious villa, the *facchino* Giuseppe leading the way. By this time the moon was well overhead, and just behind us as we tramped up the dewy lane, white in the moonlight between the ink-black hedgerows on either side. How still it was! Not a breath of air, not a sound of life; only the awful silence that had lain almost unbroken for two thousand years over this vast graveyard of a dead world.

As we passed between the shattered gates and wound our way in the moonlight through the maze of gnarled fruit-trees, decaying farm implements and piles of lumber, towards the small door that formed the only opening in the first story of this deserted fortress, the cold silence was shattered by the harsh baying of dogs somewhere in the distance to the right, beyond the barns that formed one side of the court. From the villa came neither light nor sound. Giuseppe knocked at the weather-worn door, and the sound echoed cavernously within; but there was no other reply.

He knocked again and again, and at length we heard the rasping jar of sliding bolts, and the door opened a little, showing an old, old man, bent with age and gaunt with malaria. Over his head he held a big Roman lamp, with three wicks, that cast strange shadows on his face,—a face that was harmless in its senility, but intolerably sad. He made no reply to our timid salutations, but motioned tremblingly to us to enter; and with a last "goodnight" to Giuseppe we obeyed, and stood half-way up the stone stairs that led directly from the door, while the old man tediously shot every bolt and adjusted the heavy bar.

Then we followed him in the semi-darkness up the steps into what had been the great hall of the villa. A fire was burning in a great fireplace so beautiful in design that Tom and I looked at each other with interest. By its fitful light we could see that we were in a huge circular room covered by a flat, saucer-shaped dome,—a room that must once have been superb and splendid, but that now was a lamentable wreck. The *frescoes* on the dome were stained and mildewed, and here and there the plaster was gone altogether; the carved doorways that led out on all sides had lost half the gold with which they had once been covered, and the floor was of brick, sunken into treacherous valleys.

Rough chests, piles of old newspapers, fragments of harnesses, farm implements, a heap of rusty carbines and cutlasses, nameless litter of every possible kind, made the room into a wilderness which under the firelight seemed even more picturesque than it really was. And on this inexpressible confusion of lumber the pale shapes of the seventeenth-century nymphs, startling in their weather-stained nudity, looked down with vacant smiles.

For a few moments we warmed ourselves before the fire; and then, in the same dejected silence, the old man led the way to one of the many doors, handed us a brass lamp, and with a stiff bow turned his back on us.

Once in our room alone, Tom and I looked at each other with faces that expressed the most complex emotions.

"Well, of all the rum goes," said Tom, "this is the rummiest go I ever experienced!"

"Right, my boy; as you very justly remark, we are in for it. Help me shut this door, and then we will reconnoitre, take account of stock, and size up our chances."

But the door showed no sign of closing; it grated on the brick floor and stuck in the warped casing, and it took our united efforts to jam the two inches of oak into its place, and turn the enormous old key in its rusty lock.

"Better now, much better now," said Tom; "now let us see

where we are."

The room was easily twenty-five feet square, and high in proportion; evidently it had been a state apartment, for the walls were covered with carved panelling that had once been white and gold, with mirrors in the panels, the wood now stained every imaginable colour, the mirrors cracked and broken, and dull with mildew. A big fire had just been lighted in the fireplace, the shutters were closed, and although the only furniture consisted of two massive bedsteads, and a chair with one leg shorter than the others, the room seemed almost comfortable.

I opened one of the shutters, that closed the great windows that ran from the floor almost to the ceiling, and nearly fell through the cracked glass into the floorless balcony. "Tom, come here, quick," I cried; and for a few minutes neither of us thought about our dubious surroundings, for we were looking at Pæstum by moonlight.

A flat, white mist, like water, lay over the entire meadow; from the midst rose against the blue-black sky the three ghostly temples, black and silver in the vivid moonlight, floating, it seemed, in the fog; and behind them, seen in broken glints between the pallid shafts, stretched the line of the silver sea.

Perfect silence,—the silence of implacable death.

We watched the white tide of mist rise around the temples, until we were chilled through, and so presently went to bed. There was but one door in the room, and that was securely locked; the great windows were twenty feet from the ground, so we felt reasonably safe from all possible attack.

In a few minutes Tom was asleep and breathing audibly; but my constitution is more nervous than his, and I lay awake for some little time, thinking of our curious adventure and of its possible outcome. Finally, I fell asleep,—for how long I do not know: but I woke with the feeling that someone had tried the handle of the door. The fire had fallen into a heap of coals which cast a red glow in the room, whereby I could see dimly the outline of Tom's bed, the broken-legged chair in front of the fireplace, and the door in its deep casing by the chimney, directly in front of my bed.

I sat up, nervous from my sudden awakening under these strange circumstances, and stared at the door. The latch rattled, and the door swung smoothly open. I began to shiver coldly. That door was locked; Tom and I had all we could do to jam it together and lock it. But we *did* lock it; and now it was opening silently. In a minute more it as silently closed.

Then I heard a footstep,—I swear I heard a footstep *in the room*, and with it the *froufrou* of trailing skirts; my breath stopped and my teeth grated against each other as I heard the soft footfalls and the feminine rustle pass along the room towards the fireplace. My eyes saw nothing; yet there was enough light in the room for me to distinguish the pattern on the carved panels of the door. The steps stopped by the fire, and I saw the broken-legged chair lean to the left, with a little jar as its short leg touched the floor.

I sat still, frozen, motionless, staring at the vacancy that was filled with such terror for me; and as I looked, the seat of the chair creaked, and it came back to its upright position again.

And then the footsteps came down the room lightly, towards the window; there was a pause, and then the great shutters swung back, and the white moonlight poured in. Its brilliancy was unbroken by any shadow, by any sign of material substance.

I tried to cry out, to make some sound, to awaken Tom; this sense of utter loneliness in the presence of the Inexplicable was maddening. I don't know whether my lips obeyed my will or no; at all events, Tom lay motionless, with his deaf ear up, and gave no sign.

The shutters closed as silently as they had opened; the moonlight was gone, the firelight also, and in utter darkness I waited. If I could only *see*! If something were visible, I should not mind it so much; but this ghastly hearing of every little sound, every rustle of a gown, every breath, yet seeing nothing, was soul-destroying. I think in my abject terror I prayed that I might see, only see; but the darkness was unbroken.

Then the footsteps began to waver fitfully, and I heard the

rustle of garments sliding to the floor, the clatter of little shoes flung down, the rattle of buttons, and of metal against wood.

Rigors shot over me, and my whole body shivered with collapse as I sank back on the pillow, waiting with every nerve tense, listening with all my life.

The coverlid was turned back beside me, and in another moment the great bed sank a little as something slipped between the sheets with an audible sigh.

I called to my aid every atom of remaining strength, and, with a cry that shivered between my clattering teeth, I hurled myself headlong from the bed on to the floor.

I must have lain for some time stunned and unconscious, for when I finally came to myself it was cold in the room, there was no last glow of lingering coals in the fireplace, and I was stiff with chill.

It all flashed over me like the haunting of a heavy dream. I laughed a little at the dim memory, with the thought, "I must try to recollect all the details; they will do to tell Tom," and rose stiffly to return to bed, when—there it was again, and my heart stopped,—the hand on the door.

I paused and listened. The door opened with a muffled creak, closed again, and I heard the lock turn rustily. I would have died now before getting into that bed again; but there was terror equally without; so I stood trembling and listened,—listened to heavy, stealthy steps creeping along on the other side of the bed. I clutched the coverlid, staring across into the dark.

There was a rush in the air by my face, the sound of a blow, and simultaneously a shriek, so awful, so despairing, so blood-curdling that I felt my senses leaving me again as I sank crouching on the floor by the bed.

And then began the awful duel, the duel of invisible, audible shapes; of things that shrieked and raved, mingling thin, feminine cries with low, stifled curses and indistinguishable words. Round and round the room, footsteps chasing footsteps in the ghastly night, now away by Tom's bed, now rushing swiftly down the great room until I felt the flash of swirling drapery on my hard lips. Round and round, turning and twisting till my brain whirled with the mad cries.

They were coming nearer. I felt the jar of their feet on the floor beside me. Came one long, gurgling moan close over my head, and then, crushing down upon me, the weight of a collapsing body; there was long hair over my face, and in my staring eyes; and as awful silence succeeded the less awful tumult, life went out, and I fell unfathomable miles into nothingness.

The gray dawn was sifting through the chinks in the shutters when I opened my eyes again. I lay stunned and faint, staring up at the mouldy *frescoes* on the ceiling, struggling to gather together my wandering senses and knit them into something like consciousness. But now as I pulled myself little by little together there was no thought of dreams before me. One after another the awful incidents of that unspeakable night came back, and I lay incapable of movement, of action, trying to piece together the whirling fragments of memory that circled dizzily around me.

Little by little it grew lighter in the room. I could see the pallid lines struggling through the shutters behind me, grow stronger along the broken and dusty floor. The tarnished mirrors reflected dirtily the growing daylight; a door closed, far away, and I heard the crowing of a cock; then by and by the whistle of a passing train.

Years seemed to have passed since I first came into this terrible room. I had lost the use of my tongue, my voice refused to obey my panic-stricken desire to cry out; once or twice I tried in vain to force an articulate sound through my rigid lips; and when at last a broken whisper rewarded my feverish struggles, I felt a strange sense of great victory. How soundly he slept! Ordinarily, rousing him was no easy task, and now he revolted steadily against being awakened at this untimely hour. It seemed to me that I had called him for ages almost, before I heard him grunt sleepily and turn in bed.

"Tom," I cried weakly, "Tom, come and help me!"

"What do you want? what is the matter with you?"

"Don't ask, come and help me!"

"Fallen out of bed I guess;" and he laughed drowsily.

My abject terror lest he should go to sleep again gave me new strength. Was it the actual physical paralysis born of killing fear that held me down? I could not have raised my head from the floor on my life; I could only cry out in deadly fear for Tom to come and help me.

"Why don't you get up and get into bed?" he answered, when I implored him to come to me. "You have got a bad nightmare; wake up!"

But something in my voice roused him at last, and he came chuckling across the room, stopping to throw open two of the great shutters and let a burst of white light into the room. He climbed up on the bed and peered over jeeringly. With the first glance the laugh died, and he leaped the bed and bent over me.

"My God, man, what is the matter with you? You are hurt!"

"I don't know what is the matter; lift me up, get me away from here, and I'll tell you all I know."

"But, old chap, you must be hurt awfully; the floor is covered with blood!"

He lifted my head and held me in his powerful arms. I looked down: a great red stain blotted the floor beside me.

But, apart from the black bruise on my head, there was no sign of a wound on my body, nor stain of blood on my lips. In as few words as possible I told him the whole story.

"Let's get out of this," he said when I had finished; "this is no place for us. Brigands I can stand, but—"

He helped me to dress, and as soon as possible we forced open the heavy door, the door I had seen turn so softly on its hinges only a few hours before, and came out into the great circular hall, no less strange and mysterious now in the half light of dawn than it had been by firelight. The room was empty, for it must have been very early, although a fire already blazed in the fireplace. We sat by the fire some time, seeing no one. Presently slow footsteps sounded in the stairway, and the old man entered, silent as the night before, nodding to us civilly, but showing by no sign any surprise which he may have felt at our early rising. In absolute silence he moved around, preparing coffee for us; and when at last the frugal breakfast was ready, and we sat around the rough table munching coarse bread and sipping the black coffee, he would reply to our overtures only by monosyllables.

Any attempt at drawing from him some facts as to the history of the villa was received with a grave and frigid repellence that baffled us; and we were forced to say *addio* with our hunger for some explanation of the events of the night still unsatisfied.

But we saw the temples by sunrise, when the mist-like lambent opals bathed the bases of the tall columns salmon in the morning light! It was a rhapsody in the pale and unearthly colours of Puvis de Chavannes vitalized and made glorious with splendid sunlight; the apotheosis of mist; a vision never before seen, never to be forgotten. It was so beautiful that the memory of my ghastly night paled and faded, and it was Tom who assailed the station-master with questions while we waited for the train from Agropoli.

Luckily he was more than loquacious, he was voluble under the ameliorating influence of the money we forced upon him; and this, in few words, was the story he told us while we sat on the platform smoking, marvelling at the mists that rose to the east, now veiling, now revealing the lavender Apennines.

"Is there a story of *La Villa Blanca*?"

"Ah, *Signori*, certainly; and a story very strange and very terrible. It was much time ago, a hundred,—two hundred years; I do not know. Well, the Duca di San Damiano married a lady so fair, so most beautiful that she was called *La Luna di Pesto*; but she was of the people,—more, she was of the *banditti*: her father was of Calabria, and a terror of the Campagna. But the duke was young, and he married her, and for her built the white villa; and it was a wonder throughout Campania,—you have seen? It is splendid now, even if a ruin. Well, it was less than a year after they came to the villa before the duke grew jealous,—jealous of the new captain of the *banditti* who took the place of the father of *La Luna*, himself killed in a great battle up there in the

170

mountains.

"Was there cause? Who shall know? But there were stories among the people of terrible things in the villa, and how *La Luna* was seen almost never outside the walls. Then the Duke would go for many days to Napoli, coming home only now and then to the villa that was become a fortress, so many men guarded its never-opening gates. And once—it was in the spring—the duke came silently down from Napoli, and there, by the three poplars you see away towards the north, his carriage was set upon by armed men, and he was almost killed; but he had with him many guards, and after a terrible fight the brigands were beaten off; but before him, wounded, lay the captain,—the man whom he feared and hated. He looked at him, lying there under the torchlight, and in his hand saw *his own sword*. Then he became a devil: with the same sword he ran the brigand through, leaped in the carriage, and, entering the villa, crept to the chamber of *La Luna*, and killed her with the sword she had given to her lover.

"This is all the story of the White Villa, except that the duke came never again to Pesto. He went back to the king at Napoli, and for many years he was the scourge of the *banditti* of Campania; for the king made him a general, and San Damiano was a name feared by the lawless and loved by the peaceful, until he was killed in a battle down by Mormanno.

"And *La Luna*? Some say she comes back to the villa, once a year, when the moon is full, in the month when she was slain; for the duke buried her, they say, with his own hands, in the garden that was once under the window of her chamber; and as she died unshriven, so was she buried without the pale of the church. Therefore she cannot sleep in peace,—*non è vero*? I do not know if the story is true, but this is the story, *Signori*, and there is the train for Napoli. *Ah, grazie! Signori, grazie tanto! A rivederci! Signori, a rivederci!*"

Sister Maddelena

Across the valley of the Oreto from Monreale, on the slopes of the mountains just above the little village of Parco, lies the old convent of Sta. Catarina. From the cloister terrace at Monreale you can see its pale walls and the slim campanile of its chapel rising from the crowded citron and mulberry orchards that flourish, rank and wild, no longer cared for by pious and loving hands. From the rough road that climbs the mountains to Assunto, the convent is invisible, a gnarled and ragged olive grove intervening, and a spur of cliffs as well, while from Palermo one sees only the speck of white, flashing in the sun, indistinguishable from the many similar gleams of desert monastery or pauper village.

Partly because of this seclusion, partly by reason of its extreme beauty, partly, it may be, because the present owners are more than charming and gracious in their pressing hospitality, Sta. Catarina seems to preserve an element of the poetic, almost magical; and as I drove with the Cavaliere Valguanera one evening in March out of Palermo, along the garden valley of the Oreto, then up the mountain side where the warm light of the spring sunset swept across from Monreale, lying golden and mellow on the luxuriant growth of figs, and olives, and orange-trees, and fantastic cacti, and so up to where the path of the convent swung off to the right round a dizzy point of cliff that reached out gaunt and gray from the olives below,—as I drove thus in the balmy air, and saw of a sudden a vision of creamy walls and orange roofs, draped in fantastic festoons of roses, with a single curving palm-tree stuck black and feathery against the gold sunset, it is hardly to be wondered at that I should slip into a mood of visionary enjoyment, looking for a time on the whole thing as the misty phantasm of a summer dream.

The *Cavaliere* had introduced himself to us,—Tom Rendel and me,—one morning soon after we reached Palermo, when, in the first bewilderment of architects in this paradise of art and colour, we were working nobly at our sketches in that dream of delight, the Capella Palatina. He was himself an amateur archæologist, he told us, and passionately devoted to his island; so he felt impelled to speak to any one whom he saw appreciating the almost—and in a way fortunately—unknown beauties of Palermo. In a little time we were fully acquainted, and talking like the oldest friends. Of course he knew acquaintances of Rendel's,—someone always does: this time they were officers on the tubby U. S. S. *Quinebaug*, that, during the summer of 1888, was trying to uphold the maritime honour of the United States in European waters.

Luckily for us, one of the officers was a kind of cousin of Rendel's, and came from Baltimore as well, so, as he had visited at the *Cavaliere's* place, we were soon invited to do the same. It was in this way that, with the luck that attends Rendel wherever he goes, we came to see something of domestic life in Italy, and that I found myself involved in another of those adventures for which I naturally sought so little.

I wonder if there is any other place in Sicily so faultless as Sta. Catarina? Taormina is a paradise, an epitome of all that is beautiful in Italy,—Venice excepted. Girgenti is a solemn epic, with its golden temples between the sea and hills. Cefalù is wild and strange, and Monreale a vision out of a fairy tale; but Sta. Catarina!—

Fancy a convent of creamy stone and rose-red brick perched on a ledge of rock midway between earth and heaven, the cliff falling almost sheer to the valley two hundred feet and more, the mountain rising behind straight towards the sky; all the rocks covered with cactus and dwarf fig-trees, the convent draped in smothering roses, and in front a terrace with a fountain in the midst; and then—nothing—between you and the sapphire sea, six miles away. Below stretches the Eden valley, the Concha d'Oro, gold-green fig orchards alternating with smoke-blue olives, the mountains rising on either hand and sinking undulously away towards the bay where, like a magic city of ivory and nacre, Palermo lies guarded by the twin mountains, Monte Pellegrino and Capo Zafferano, arid rocks like dull amethysts, rose in sunlight, violet in shadow: lions *couchant*, guarding the sleeping town.

Seen as we saw it for the first time that hot evening in March, with the golden lambent light pouring down through the valley, making it in verity a "shell of gold," sitting in Indian chairs on the terrace, with the perfume of roses and jasmines all around us, the valley of the Oreto, Palermo, Sta. Catarina, Monreale,- all were but parts of a dreamy vision, like the heavenly city of Sir Percivale, to attain which he passed across the golden bridge that burned after him as he vanished in the intolerable light of the Beatific Vision.

It was all so unreal, so phantasmal, that I was not surprised in the least when, late in the evening after the ladies had gone to their rooms, and the *Cavaliere*, Tom, and I were stretched out in chairs on the terrace, smoking lazily under the multitudinous stars, the *Cavaliere* said, "There is something I really must tell you both before you go to bed, so that you may be spared any unnecessary alarm."

"You are going to say that the place is haunted," said Rendel, feeling vaguely on the floor beside him for his glass of Amaro: "thank you; it is all it needs."

The *Cavaliere* smiled a little: "Yes, that is just it. Sta. Catarina is really haunted; and much as my reason revolts against the idea as superstitious and savouring of priestcraft, yet I must acknowledge I see no way of avoiding the admission. I do not presume to offer any explanations, I only state the fact; and the fact is that tonight one or other of you will, in all human—or unhuman- probability, receive a visit from Sister Maddelena. You need not

174

be in the least afraid, the apparition is perfectly gentle and harm-less; and, moreover, having seen it once, you will never see it again. No one sees the ghost, or whatever it is, but once, and that usually the first night he spends in the house. I myself saw the thing eight—nine years ago, when I first bought the place from the Marchese di Muxaro; all my people have seen it, nearly all my guests, so I think you may as well be prepared."

"Then tell us what to expect," I said; "what kind of a ghost is this nocturnal visitor?"

"It is simple enough. Sometime tonight you will suddenly awake and see before you a Carmelite nun who will look fix-edly at you, say distinctly and very sadly, 'I cannot sleep,' and then vanish. That is all, it is hardly worth speaking of, only some people are terribly frightened if they are visited unwarned by strange apparitions; so I tell you this that you may be prepared."

"This was a Carmelite convent, then?" I said.

"Yes; it was suppressed after the unification of Italy, and given to the House of Muxaro; but the family died out, and I bought it. There is a story about the ghostly nun, who was only a novice, and even that unwillingly, which gives an interest to an other-wise very commonplace and uninteresting ghost."

"I beg that you will tell it us," cried Rendel.

"There is a storm coming," I added. "See, the lightning is flashing already up among the mountains at the head of the val-ley; if the story is tragic, as it must be, now is just the time for it. You will tell it, will you not?"

The *Cavaliere* smiled that slow, cryptic smile of his that was so unfathomable.

"As you say, there is a shower coming, and as we have fierce tempests here, we might not sleep; so perhaps we may as well sit up a little longer, and I will tell you the story."

The air was utterly still, hot and oppressive; the rich, sick odour of the oranges just bursting into bloom came up from the valley in a gently rising tide. The sky, thick with stars, seemed mirrored in the rich foliage below, so numerous were the glow-worms under the still trees, and the fireflies that gleamed in the hot air. Lightning flashed fitfully from the darkening west; but as yet no thunder broke the heavy silence.

The *Cavaliere* lighted another cigar, and pulled a cushion under his head so that he could look down to the distant lights of the city. "This is the story," he said.

"Once upon a time, late in the last century, the Duca di Castiglione was attached to the court of Charles III., King of the Two Sicilies, down at Palermo. They tell me he was very ambitious, and, not content with marrying his son to one of the ladies of the House of Tuscany, had betrothed his only daughter, Rosalia, to Prince Antonio, a cousin of the king. His whole life was wrapped up in the fame of his family, and he quite forgot all domestic affection in his madness for dynastic glory. His son was a worthy scion, cold and proud; but Rosalia was, according to legend, utterly the reverse,—a passionate, beautiful girl, wilful and headstrong, and careless of her family and the world.

"The time had nearly come for her to marry Prince Antonio, a typical *roué* of the Spanish court, when, through the treachery of a servant, the duke discovered that his daughter was in love with a young military officer whose name I don't remember, and that an elopement had been planned to take place the next night. The fury and dismay of the old autocrat passed belief; he saw in a flash the downfall of all his hopes of family aggrandizement through union with the royal house, and, knowing well the spirit of his daughter, despaired of ever bringing her to subjection.

"Nevertheless, he attacked her unmercifully, and, by bullying and threats, by imprisonment, and even bodily chastisement, he tried to break her spirit and bend her to his indomitable will. Through his power at court he had the lover sent away to the mainland, and for more than a year he held his daughter closely imprisoned in his palace on the Toledo,—that one, you may remember, on the right, just beyond the *Via del Collegio dei Gesuiti*, with the beautiful iron-work grilles at all the windows, and the painted frieze.

"But nothing could move her, nothing bend her stubborn

will; and at last, furious at the girl he could not govern, Castiglione sent her to this convent, then one of the few houses of barefoot Carmelite nuns in Italy. He stipulated that she should take the name of Maddelena, that he should never hear of her again, and that she should be held an absolute prisoner in this conventual castle.

"Rosalia—or Sister Maddelena, as she was now—believed her lover dead, for her father had given her good proofs of this, and she believed him; nevertheless she refused to marry another, and seized upon the convent life as a blessed relief from the tyranny of her maniacal father.

"She lived here for four or five years; her name was forgotten at court and in her father's palace. Rosalia di Castiglione was dead, and only Sister Maddelena lived, a Carmelite nun, in her place.

"In 1798 Ferdinand IV. found himself driven from his throne on the mainland, his kingdom divided, and he himself forced to flee to Sicily. With him came the lover of the dead Rosalia, now high in military honour. He on his part had thought Rosalia dead, and it was only by accident that he found that she still lived, a Carmelite nun.

"Then began the second act of the romance that until then had been only sadly commonplace, but now became dark and tragic. Michele—Michele Biscari,—that was his name; I remember now—haunted the region of the convent, striving to communicate with Sister Maddelena; and at last, from the cliffs over us, up there among the citrons—you will see by the next flash of lightning—he saw her in the great cloister, recognized her in her white habit, found her the same dark and splendid beauty of six years before, only made more beautiful by her white habit and her rigid life.

"By and by he found a day when she was alone, and tossed a ring to her as she stood in the midst of the cloister. She looked up, saw him, and from that moment lived only to love him in life as she had loved his memory in the death she had thought had overtaken him.

"With the utmost craft they arranged their plans together. They could not speak, for a word would have aroused the other inmates of the convent. They could make signs only when Sister Maddelena was alone. Michele could throw notes to her from the cliff,—a feat demanding a strong arm, as you will see, if you measure the distance with your eye,—and she could drop replies from the window over the cliff, which he picked up at the bottom.

"Finally he succeeded in casting into the cloister a coil of light rope. The girl fastened it to the bars of one of the windows, and—so great is the madness of love—Biscari actually climbed the rope from the valley to the window of the cell, a distance of almost two hundred feet, with but three little craggy resting-places in all that height. For nearly a month these nocturnal visits were undiscovered, and Michele had almost completed his arrangements for carrying the girl from Sta. Catarina and away to Spain, when unfortunately one of the sisters, suspecting some mystery, from the changed face of Sister Maddelena, began investigating, and at length discovered the rope neatly coiled up by the nun's window, and hidden under some clinging vines.

"She instantly told the Mother Superior; and together they watched from a window in the crypt of the chapel,—the only place, as you will see tomorrow, from which one could see the window of Sister Maddelena's cell. They saw the figure of Michele daringly ascending the slim rope; watched hour after hour, the Sister remaining while the Superior went to say the hours in the chapel, at each of which Sister Maddelena was present; and at last, at prime, just as the sun was rising, they saw the figure slip down the rope, watched the rope drawn up and concealed, and knew that Sister Maddelena was in their hands for vengeance and punishment,—a criminal.

"The next day, by the order of the Mother Superior, Sister Maddelena was imprisoned in one of the cells under the chapel, charged with her guilt, and commanded to make full and complete confession. But not a word would she say, although they offered her forgiveness if she would tell the name of her lover.

At last the Superior told her that after this fashion would they act the coming night: she herself would be placed in the crypt, tied in front of the window, her mouth gagged; that the rope would be lowered, and the lover allowed to approach even to the sill of her window, and at that moment the rope would be cut, and before her eyes her lover would be dashed to death on the ragged cliffs.

"The plan was feasible, and Sister Maddelena knew that the Mother was perfectly capable of carrying it out. Her stubborn spirit was broken, and in the only way possible; she begged for mercy, for the sparing of her lover. The Mother Superior was deaf at first; at last she said, 'It is your life or his. I will spare him on condition that you sacrifice your own life.' Sister Maddelena accepted the terms joyfully, wrote a last farewell to Michele, fastened the note to the rope, and with her own hands cut the rope and saw it fall coiling down to the valley bed far below.

"Then she silently prepared for death; and at midnight, while her lover was wandering, mad with the horror of impotent fear, around the white walls of the convent, Sister Maddelena, for love of Michele, gave up her life. How, was never known. That she was indeed dead was only a suspicion, for when Biscari finally compelled the civil authorities to enter the convent, claiming that murder had been done there, they found no sign. Sister Maddelena had been sent to the parent house of the barefoot Carmelites at Avila in Spain, so the Superior stated, because of her incorrigible contumacy.

"The old Duke of Castiglione refused to stir hand or foot in the matter, and Michele, after fruitless attempts to prove that the Superior of Sta. Catarina had caused the death, was forced to leave Sicily. He sought in Spain for very long; but no sign of the girl was to be found, and at last he died, exhausted with suffering and sorrow.

"Even the name of Sister Maddelena was forgotten, and it was not until the convents were suppressed, and this house came into the hands of the Muxaros, that her story was remembered. It was then that the ghost began to appear; and, an explanation being necessary, the story, or legend, was obtained from one of the nuns who still lived after the suppression. I think the fact—for it is a fact—of the ghost rather goes to prove that Michele was right, and that poor Rosalia gave her life a sacrifice for love,—whether in accordance with the terms of the legend or not, I cannot say. One or the other of you will probably see her tonight. You might ask her for the facts. Well, that is all the story of Sister Maddelena, known in the world as Rosalia di Castiglione. Do you like it?"

"It is admirable," said Rendel, enthusiastically. "But I fancy I should rather look on it simply as a story, and not as a warning of what is going to happen. I don't much fancy real ghosts myself."

"But the poor Sister is quite harmless;" and Valguanera rose, stretching himself. "My servants say she wants a mass said over her, or something of that kind; but I haven't much love for such priestly hocus-pocus,—I beg your pardon" (turning to me), "I had forgotten that you were a Catholic: forgive my rudeness."

"My dear *Cavaliere*, I beg you not to apologize. I am sorry you cannot see things as I do; but don't for a moment think I am hypersensitive."

"I have an excuse,—perhaps you will say only an explanation; but I live where I see all the absurdities and corruptions of the church."

"Perhaps you let the accidents blind you to the essentials; but do not let us quarrel tonight,—see, the storm is close on us. Shall we go in?"

The stars were blotted out through nearly all the sky; low, thunderous clouds, massed at the head of the valley, were sweeping over so close that they seemed to brush the black pines on the mountain above us. To the south and east the storm-clouds had shut down almost to the sea, leaving a space of black sky where the moon in its last quarter was rising just to the left of Monte Pellegrino,—a black silhouette against the pallid moonlight. The rosy lightning flashed almost incessantly, and through the fitful darkness came the sound of bells across the valley, the rushing torrent below, and the dull roar of the approaching rain, with a deep organ point of solemn thunder through it all.

We fled indoors from the coming tempest, and taking our candles, said "goodnight," and sought each his respective room.

My own was in the southern part of the old convent, giving on the terrace we had just quitted, and about over the main doorway. The rushing storm, as it swept down the valley with the swelling torrent beneath, was very fascinating, and after wrapping myself in a dressing-gown I stood for some time by the deeply embrasured window, watching the blazing lightning and the beating rain whirled by fitful gusts of wind around the spurs of the mountains. Gradually the violence of the shower seemed to decrease, and I threw myself down on my bed in the hot air, wondering if I really was to experience the ghostly visit the *Cavaliere* so confidently predicted.

I had thought out the whole matter to my own satisfaction, and fancied I knew exactly what I should do, in case Sister Maddelena came to visit me. The story touched me: the thought of the poor faithful girl who sacrificed herself for her lover,—himself, very likely, quite unworthy,—and who now could never sleep for reason of her unquiet soul, sent out into the storm of eternity without spiritual aid or counsel. I could not sleep; for the still vivid lightning, the crowding thoughts of the dead nun, and the shivering anticipation of my possible visitation, made slumber quite out of the question.

No suspicion of sleepiness had visited me, when, perhaps an hour after midnight, came a sudden vivid flash of lightning, and, as my dazzled eyes began to regain the power of sight, I saw her as plainly as in life,—a tall figure, shrouded in the white habit of the Carmelites, her head bent, her hands clasped before her. In another flash of lightning she slowly raised her head and looked at me long and earnestly. She was very beautiful, like the Virgin of Beltraffio in the National Gallery,—more beautiful than I had supposed possible, her deep, passionate eyes very tender and pitiful in their pleading, beseeching glance. I hardly think I was frightened, or even startled, but lay looking steadily at her as she stood in the beating lightning.

Then she breathed, rather than articulated, with a voice that almost brought tears, so infinitely sad and sorrowful was it, "I cannot sleep!" and the liquid eyes grew more pitiful and questioning as bright tears fell from them down the pale dark face.

The figure began to move slowly towards the door, its eyes fixed on mine with a look that was weary and almost agonized. I leaped from the bed and stood waiting. A look of utter gratitude swept over the face, and, turning, the figure passed through the doorway.

Out into the shadow of the corridor it moved, like a drift of pallid storm-cloud, and I followed, all natural and instinctive fear or nervousness quite blotted out by the part I felt I was to play in giving rest to a tortured soul. The corridors were velvet black; but the pale figure floated before me always, an unerring guide, now but a thin mist on the utter night, now white and clear in the bluish lightning through some window or doorway.

Down the stairway into the lower hall, across the refectory, where the great *frescoed* crucifixion flared into sudden clearness under the fitful lightning, out into the silent cloister.

It was very dark. I stumbled along the heaving bricks, now guiding myself by a hand on the whitewashed wall, now by a touch on a column wet with the storm. From all the eaves the rain was dripping on to the pebbles at the foot of the arcade: a pigeon, startled from the capital where it was sleeping, beat its way into the cloister close. Still the white thing drifted before me to the farther side of the court, then along the cloister at right angles, and paused before one of the many doorways that led to the cells.

A sudden blaze of fierce lightning, the last now of the fleeting trail of storm, leaped around us, and in the vivid light I saw the white face turned again with the look of overwhelming desire, of beseeching *pathos*, that had choked my throat with an involuntary sob when first I saw Sister Maddelena. In the brief interval that ensued after the flash, and before the roaring thunder burst like the crash of battle over the trembling convent, I

182

heard again the sorrowful words, "I cannot sleep," come from the impenetrable darkness. And when the lightning came again, the white figure was gone.

I wandered around the courtyard, searching in vain for Sister Maddelena, even until the moonlight broke through the torn and sweeping fringes of the storm. I tried the door where the white figure vanished: it was locked; but I had found what I sought, and, carefully noting its location, went back to my room, but not to sleep.

In the morning the *Cavaliere* asked Rendel and me which of us had seen the ghost, and I told him my story; then I asked him to grant me permission to sift the thing to the bottom; and he courteously gave the whole matter into my charge, promising that he would consent to anything.

I could hardly wait to finish breakfast; but no sooner was this done than, forgetting my morning pipe, I started with Rendel and the *Cavaliere* to investigate.

"I am sure there is nothing in that cell," said Valguanera, when we came in front of the door I had marked. "It is curious that you should have chosen the door of the very cell that tradition assigns to Sister Maddelena; but I have often examined that room myself, and I am sure that there is no chance for anything to be concealed. In fact, I had the floor taken up once, soon after I came here, knowing the room was that of the mysterious Sister, and thinking that there, if anywhere, the monastic crime would have taken place; still, we will go in, if you like."

He unlocked the door, and we entered, one of us, at all events, with a beating heart. The cell was very small, hardly eight feet square. There certainly seemed no opportunity for concealing a body in the tiny place; and although I sounded the floor and walls, all gave a solid, heavy answer,—the unmistakable sound of masonry.

For the innocence of the floor the *Cavaliere* answered. He had, he said, had it all removed, even to the curving surfaces of the vault below; yet somewhere in this room the body of the murdered girl was concealed,—of this I was certain. But where? There seemed no answer; and I was compelled to give up the search for the moment, somewhat to the amusement of Valguanera, who had watched curiously to see if I could solve the mystery.

But I could not forget the subject, and towards noon started on another tour of investigation. I procured the keys from the *Cavaliere*, and examined the cells adjoining; they were apparently the same, each with its window opposite the door, and nothing—Stay, were they the same? I hastened into the suspected cell; it was as I thought: this cell, being on the corner, could have had two windows, yet only one was visible, and that to the left, at right angles with the doorway. Was it imagination? As I sounded the wall opposite the door, where the other window should be, I fancied that the sound was a trifle less solid and dull. I was becoming excited. I dashed back to the cell on the right, and, forcing open the little window, thrust my head out.

It was found at last! In the smooth surface of the yellow wall was a rough space, following approximately the shape of the other cell windows, not plastered like the rest of the wall, but showing the shapes of bricks through its thick coatings of whitewash. I turned with a gasp of excitement and satisfaction: yes, the embrasure of the wall was deep enough; what a wall it was!—four feet at least, and the opening of the window reached to the floor, though the window itself was hardly three feet square. I felt absolutely certain that the secret was solved, and called the *Cavaliere* and Rendel, too excited to give them an explanation of my theories.

They must have thought me mad when I suddenly began scraping away at the solid wall in front of the door; but in a few minutes they understood what I was about, for under the coatings of paint and plaster appeared the original bricks; and as my architectural knowledge had led me rightly, the space I had cleared was directly over a vertical joint between firm, workmanlike masonry on one hand, and rough amateurish work on the other, bricks laid anyway, and without order or science.

Rendel seized a pick, and was about to assail the rude wall, when I stopped him.

"Let us be careful," I said; "who knows what we may find?" So we set to work digging out the mortar around a brick at about the level of our eyes.

How hard the mortar had become! But a brick yielded at last, and with trembling fingers I detached it. Darkness within, yet beyond question there was a cavity there, not a solid wall; and with infinite care we removed another brick. Still the hole was too small to admit enough light from the dimly illuminated cell. With a chisel we pried at the sides of a large block of masonry, perhaps eight bricks in size. It moved, and we softly slid it from its bed.

Valguanera, who was standing watching us as we lowered the bricks to the floor, gave a sudden cry, a cry like that of a frightened woman,—terrible, coming from him. Yet there was cause.

Framed by the ragged opening of the bricks, hardly seen in the dim light, was a face, an ivory image, more beautiful than any antique bust, but drawn and distorted by unspeakable agony: the lovely mouth half open, as though gasping for breath; the eyes cast upward; and below, slim chiselled hands crossed on the breast, but clutching the folds of the white Carmelite habit, torture and agony visible in every tense muscle, fighting against the determination of the rigid pose.

We stood there breathless, staring at the pitiful sight, fascinated, bewitched. So this was the secret. With fiendish ingenuity, the rigid ecclesiastics had blocked up the window, then forced the beautiful creature to stand in the alcove, while with remorseless hands and iron hearts they had shut her into a living tomb. I had read of such things in romance; but to find the verity here, before my eyes—

Steps came down the cloister, and with a simultaneous thought we sprang to the door and closed it behind us. The room was sacred; that awful sight was not for curious eyes. The gardener was coming to ask some trivial question of Valguanera. The *Cavaliere* cut him short. "Pietro, go down to Parco and ask Padre Stefano to come here at once." (I thanked him with

185

a glance.) "Stay!" He turned to me: "*Signore*, it is already two o'clock and too late for mass, is it not?"

I nodded.

Valguanera thought a moment, then he said, "Bring two horses; the *Signor Americano* will go with you,—do you understand?" Then, turning to me, "You will go, will you not? I think you can explain matters to Padre Stefano better than I."

"Of course I will go, more than gladly." So it happened that after a hasty luncheon I wound down the mountain to Parco, found Padre Stefano, explained my errand to him, found him intensely eager and sympathetic, and by five o'clock had him back at the convent with all that was necessary for the resting of the soul of the dead girl.

In the warm twilight, with the last light of the sunset pouring into the little cell through the window where almost a century ago Rosalia had for the last time said farewell to her lover, we gathered together to speed her tortured soul on its journey, so long delayed. Nothing was omitted; all the needful offices of the church were said by Padre Stefano, while the light in the window died away, and the flickering flames of the candles carried by two of the acolytes from San Francesco threw fitful flashes of pallid light into the dark recess where the white face had prayed to Heaven for a hundred years.

Finally, the *Padre* took the *asperge* from the hands of one of the *acolytes*, and with a sign of the cross in benediction while he chanted the *Asperges*, gently sprinkled the holy water on the upturned face. Instantly the whole vision crumbled to dust, the face was gone, and where once the candlelight had flickered on the perfect semblance of the girl dead so very long, it now fell only on the rough bricks which closed the window, bricks laid with frozen hearts by pitiless hands.

But our task was not done yet. It had been arranged that Padre Stefano should remain at the convent all night, and that as soon as midnight made it possible he should say the first mass for the repose of the girl's soul. We sat on the terrace talking over the strange events of the last crowded hours, and I noted with satisfaction that the *Cavaliere* no longer spoke of the church with that hardness, which had hurt me so often. It is true that the *Padre* was with us nearly all the time; but not only was Valguanera courteous, he was almost sympathetic; and I wondered if it might not prove that more than one soul benefited by the untoward events of the day.

With the aid of the astonished and delighted servants, and no little help as well from Signora Valguanera, I fitted up the long cold Altar in the chapel, and by midnight we had the gloomy sanctuary beautiful with flowers and candles. It was a curiously solemn service, in the first hour of the new day, in the midst of blazing candles and the thick incense, the odour of the opening orange-blooms drifting up in the fresh morning air, and mingling with the incense smoke and the perfume of flowers within.

Many prayers were said that night for the soul of the dead girl, and I think many afterwards; for after the benediction I remained for a little time in my place, and when I rose from my knees and went towards the chapel door, I saw a figure kneeling still, and, with a start, recognized the form of the *Cavaliere*. I smiled with quiet satisfaction and gratitude, and went away softly, content with the chain of events that now seemed finished.

The next day the alcove was again walled up, for the precious dust could not be gathered together for transportation to consecrated ground; so I went down to the little cemetery at Parco for a basket of earth, which we cast in over the ashes of Sister Maddelena.

By and by, when Rendel and I went away, with great regret, Valguanera came down to Palermo with us; and the last act that we performed in Sicily was assisting him to order a tablet of marble, whereon was carved this simple inscription:—

Here Lies The Body Of
Rosalia Di Castiglioni,
Called
Sister Maddelena.

Her Soul
Is With Him Who Gave It.

To this I added in thought:—

"Let him that is without sin among you cast the first stone."

Notre Dame des Eaux

West of St. Pol de Leon, on the sea-cliffs of Finisterre, stands the ancient church of Notre Dame des Eaux. Five centuries of beating winds and sweeping rains have moulded its angles, and worn its carvings and sculpture down to the very semblance of the ragged cliffs themselves, until even the Breton fisherman, looking lovingly from his boat as he makes for the harbour of Morlaix, hardly can say where the crags end, and where the church begins.

The teeth of the winds of the sea have devoured, bit by bit, the fine sculpture of the doorway and the thin cusps of the window tracery; gray moss creeps caressingly over the worn walls in ineffectual protection; gentle vines, turned crabbed by the harsh beating of the fierce winds, clutch the crumbling buttresses, climb up over the sinking roof, reach in even at the louvres of the belfry, holding the little sanctuary safe in desperate arms against the savage warfare of the sea and sky.

Many a time you may follow the rocky highway from St. Pol even around the last land of France, and so to Brest, yet never see sign of Notre Dame des Eaux; for it clings to a cliff somewhat lower than the road, and between grows a stunted thicket of harsh and ragged trees, their skeleton white branches, tortured and contorted, thrusting sorrowfully out of the hard, dark foliage that still grows below, where the rise of land below the highway gives some protection. You must leave the wood by the two cottages of yellow stone, about twenty miles beyond St. Pol, and go down to the right, around the old stone quarry; then, bearing to the left by the little cliff path, you will, in a moment, see the pointed roof of the tower of Notre Dame, and, later, come down to the side porch among the crosses of the arid little graveyard.

It is worth the walk, for though the church has outwardly little but its sad picturesqueness to repay the artist, within it is a dream and a delight. A Norman nave of round, red stone piers and arches, a delicate choir of the richest flamboyant, a High Altar of the time of Francis I., form only the mellow background and frame for carven tombs and dark old pictures, hanging lamps of iron and brass, and black, heavily carved choir-stalls of the Renaissance.

So has the little church lain unnoticed for many centuries; for the horrors and follies of the Revolution have never come near, and the hardy and faithful people of Finisterre have feared God and loved Our Lady too well to harm her church. For many years it was the church of the Comtes de Jarleuc; and these are their tombs that mellow year by year under the warm light of the painted windows, given long ago by Comte Robert de Jarleuc, when the heir of Poullaouen came safely to shore in the harbour of Morlaix, having escaped from the Isle of Wight, where he had lain captive after the awful defeat of the fleet of Charles of Valois at Sluys. And now the heir of Poullaouen lies in a carven tomb, forgetful of the world where he fought so nobly: the dynasty he fought to establish, only a memory; the family he made glorious, a name; the Château Poullaouen a single crag of riven masonry in the fields of M. du Bois, mayor of Morlaix.

It was Julien, Comte de Bergerac, who rediscovered Notre Dame des Eaux, and by his picture of its dreamy interior in the Salon of '86 brought once more into notice this forgotten corner of the world. The next year a party of painters settled themselves nearby, roughing it as best they could, and in the year following, Mme. de Bergerac and her daughter Héloïse came with Julien, and, buying the old farm of Pontivy, on the highway over Notre Dame, turned it into a summer house that almost made amends for their lost *château* on the Dordogne, stolen from them as virulent Royalists by the triumphant Republic in 1794.

Little by little a summer colony of painters gathered around Pontivy, and it was not until the spring of 1890 that the peace of the colony was broken. It was a sorrowful tragedy. Jean d'Yriex, the youngest and merriest devil of all the jolly crew, became suddenly moody and morose. At first this was attributed to his undisguised admiration for Mlle. Héloïse, and was looked on as one of the vagaries of boyish passion; but one day, while riding with M. de Bergerac, he suddenly seized the bridle of Julien's horse, wrenched it from his hand, and, turning his own horse's head towards the cliffs, lashed the terrified animals into a gallop straight towards the brink.

He was only thwarted in his mad object by Julien, who with a quick blow sent him headlong in the dry grass, and reined in the terrified animals hardly a yard from the cliffs. When this happened, and no word of explanation was granted, only a sullen silence that lasted for days, it became clear that poor Jean's brain was wrong in some way. Héloïse devoted herself to him with infinite patience,—though she felt no special affection for him, only pity,—and while he was with her he seemed sane and quiet. But at night some strange mania took possession of him. If he had worked on his Prix de Rome picture in the daytime, while Héloïse sat by him, reading aloud or singing a little, no matter how good the work, it would have vanished in the morning, and he would again begin, only to erase his labor during the night.

At last his growing insanity reached its climax; and one day in Notre Dame, when he had painted better than usual, he suddenly stopped, seized a palette knife, and slashed the great canvas in strips. Héloïse sprang forward to stop him, and in crazy fury he turned on her, striking at her throat with the palette knife. The thin steel snapped, and the white throat showed only a scarlet scratch. Héloïse, without that ordinary terror that would crush most women, grasped the thin wrists of the madman, and, though he could easily have wrenched his hands away, d'Yriex sank on his knees in a passion of tears.

He shut himself in his room at Pontivy, refusing to see any one, walking for hours up and down, fighting against growing madness. Soon Dr. Charpentier came from Paris, summoned by Mme. de Bergerac; and after one short, forced interview, left at once for Paris, taking M. d'Yriex with him.

A few days later came a letter for Mme. de Bergerac, in which Dr. Charpentier confessed that Jean had disappeared, that he had allowed him too much liberty, owing to his apparent calmness, and that when the train stopped at Le Mans he had slipped from him and utterly vanished.

During the summer, word came occasionally that no trace had been found of the unhappy man, and at last the Pontivy colony realized that the merry boy was dead. Had he lived he *must* have been found, for the exertions of the police were perfect; yet not the slightest trace was discovered, and his lamentable death was acknowledged, not only by Mme. de Bergerac and Jean's family,—sorrowing for the death of their first-born, away in the warm hills of Lozère,—but by Dr. Charpentier as well.

So the summer passed, and the autumn came, and at last the cold rains of November—the skirmish line of the advancing army of winter—drove the colony back to Paris.

It was the last day at Pontivy, and Mlle. Héloïse had come down to Notre Dame for a last look at the beautiful shrine, a last prayer for the repose of the tortured soul of poor Jean d'Yriex. The rains had ceased for a time, and a warm stillness lay over the cliffs and on the creeping sea, swaying and lapping around the ragged shore. Héloïse knelt very long before the Altar of Our Lady of the Waters; and when she finally rose, could not bring herself to leave as yet that place of sorrowful beauty, all warm and golden with the last light of the declining sun. She watched the old verger, Pierre Polou, stumping softly around the darkening building, and spoke to him once, asking the hour; but he was very deaf, as well as nearly blind, and he did not answer.

So she sat in the corner of the aisle by the Altar of Our Lady of the Waters, watching the checkered light fade in the advancing shadows, dreaming sad daydreams of the dead summer, until the daydreams merged in night-dreams, and she fell asleep.

Then the last light of the early sunset died in the gleaming

quarries of the west window; Pierre Polou stumbled uncertain-
ly through the dusky shadow, locked the sagging doors of the
mouldering south porch, and took his way among the leaning
crosses up to the highway and his little cottage, a good mile
away,—the nearest house to the lonely church of Notre Dame
des Eaux.

With the setting of the sun great clouds rose swiftly from the
sea; the wind freshened, and the gaunt branches of the weather-
worn trees in the churchyard lashed themselves beseechingly
before the coming storm. The tide turned, and the waters at
the foot of the rocks swept uneasily up the narrow beach and
caught at the weary cliffs, their sobbing growing and deepening
to a threatening, solemn roar. Whirls of dead leaves rose in the
churchyard, and threw themselves against the blank windows.
The winter and the night came down together.

Héloïse awoke, bewildered and wondering; in a moment she
realized the situation, and without fear or uneasiness. There was
nothing to dread in Notre Dame by night; the ghosts, if there
were ghosts, would not trouble her, and the doors were securely locked. It was foolish of her to fall asleep, and her mother
would be most uneasy at Pontivy if she realized before dawn
that Héloïse had not returned.

On the other hand, she was in the habit of wandering off to
walk after dinner, often not coming home until late, so it was
quite possible that she might return before *Madame* knew of her
absence, for Polou came always to unlock the church for the
low mass at six o'clock; so she arose from her cramped position
in the aisle, and walked slowly up to the choir-rail, entered the
chancel, and felt her way to one of the stalls, on the south side,
where there were cushions and an easy back.

It was really very beautiful in Notre Dame by night; she had
never suspected how strange and solemn the little church could
be when the moon shone fitfully through the south windows,
now bright and clear, now blotted out by sweeping clouds. The
nave was barred with the long shadows of the heavy pillars, and
when the moon came out she could see far down almost to the

west end. How still it was! Only a soft low murmur without of the restless limbs of the trees, and of the creeping sea.

It was very soothing, almost like a song; and Héloïse felt sleep coming back to her as the clouds shut out the moon, and all the church grew black.

She was drifting off into the last delicious moment of vanishing consciousness, when she suddenly came fully awake, with a shock that made every nerve tingle. In the midst of the far faint sounds of the tempestuous night she had heard a footstep! Yet the church was utterly empty, she was sure. And again! A footstep dragging and uncertain, stealthy and cautious, but an unmistakable step, away in the blackest shadow at the end of the church.

She sat up, frozen with the fear that comes at night and that is overwhelming, her hands clutching the coarse carving of the arms of the stall, staring down into the dark.

Again the footstep, and again,—slow, measured, one after another at intervals of perhaps half a minute, growing a little louder each time, a little nearer.

Would the darkness never be broken? Would the cloud never pass? Minute after minute went like weary hours, and still the moon was hid, still the dead branches rattled clatteringly on the high windows. Unconsciously she moved, as under a magician's spell, down to the choir-rail, straining her eyes to pierce the thick night. And the step, it was very near! Ah, the moon at last! A white ray fell through the westernmost window, painting a bar of light on the floor of sagging stone. Then a second bar, then a third, and a fourth, and for a moment Héloïse could have cried out with relief, for nothing broke the lines of light,—no figure, no shadow.

In another moment came a step, and from the shadow of the last column appeared in the pallid moonlight the figure of a man. The girl stared breathless, the moonlight falling on her as she stood rigid against the low parapet. Another step and another, and she saw before her—was it ghost or living man?—a white mad face staring from matted hair and beard, a tall thin figure half clothed in rags, limping as it stepped towards her with wounded feet. From the dead face stared mad eyes that gleamed like the eyes of a cat, fixed on hers with insane persistence, holding her, fascinating her as a cat fascinates a bird.

One more step,—it was close before her now! those awful, luminous eyes dilating and contracting in awful palpitations. And the moon was going out; the shadows swept one by one over the windows; she stared at the moonlit face for a last fascinated glance—Mother of God! it was—— The shadow swept over them, and now only remained the blazing eyes and the dim outline of a form that crouched waveringly before her as a cat crouches, drawing its vibrating body together for the spring that blots out the life of the victim.

In another instant the mad thing would leap; but just as the quiver swept over the crouching body, Héloïse gathered all her strength into one action of desperate terror.

"Jean, stop!"

The thing crouched before her paused, chattering softly to itself; then it articulated dryly, and with all the trouble of a learning child, the one word, "*Chantez!*"

Without a thought, Héloïse sang; it was the first thing that she remembered, an old Provençal song that d'Yriex had always loved. While she sang, the poor mad creature lay huddled at her feet, separated from her only by the choir parapet, its dilating, contracting eyes never moving for an instant. As the song died away, came again that awful tremor, indicative of the coming death-spring, and again she sang,—this time the old *Pange lingua*, its sonorous Latin sounding in the deserted church like the voice of dead centuries.

And so she sang, on and on, hour after hour,—hymns and *chansons*, folk-songs and bits from comic operas, songs of the boulevards alternating with the *Tantum ergo* and the *O Filii et Filiæ*. It mattered little what she sang. At last it seemed to her that it mattered little whether she sang or no; for her brain whirled round and round like a dizzy *maelstrom*, her icy hands, griping the hard rail, alone supported her dying body. She could hear no sound of her song; her body was numb, her mouth parched, her lips cracked and bleeding; she felt the drops of blood fall from her chin. And still she sang, with the yellow palpitating eyes holding her as in a vice.

If only she could continue until dawn! It must be dawn so soon! The windows were growing gray, the rain lashed outside, she could distinguish the features of the horror before her; but the night of death was growing with the coming day, blackness swept down upon her; she could sing no more, her tortured lips made one last effort to form the words, "Mother of God, save me!" and night and death came down like a crushing wave.

But her prayer was heard; the dawn had come, and Polou unlocked the porch-door for Father Augustin just in time to hear the last agonized cry. The maniac turned in the very act of leaping on his victim, and sprang for the two men, who stopped in dumb amazement. Poor old Pierre Polou went down at a blow; but Father Augustin was young and fearless, and he grappled the mad animal with all his strength and will. It would have gone ill even with him,—for no one can stand against the bestial fury of a man in whom reason is dead,—had not some sudden impulse seized the maniac, who pitched the priest aside with a single movement, and, leaping through the door, vanished forever.

Did he hurl himself from the cliffs in the cold wet morning, or was he doomed to wander, a wild beast, until, captured, he beat himself in vain against the walls of some asylum, an unknown pauper lunatic? None ever knew.

The colony at Pontivy was blotted out by the dreary tragedy, and Notre Dame des Eaux sank once more into silence and solitude. Once a year Father Augustin said mass for the repose of the soul of Jean d'Yriex; but no other memory remained of the horror that blighted the lives of an innocent girl and of a gray-haired mother mourning for her dead boy in far Lozère.

The Dead Valley

I have a friend, Olof Ehrensvärd, a Swede by birth, who yet, by reason of a strange and melancholy mischance of his early boyhood, has thrown his lot with that of the New World. It is a curious story of a headstrong boy and a proud and relentless family: the details do not matter here, but they are sufficient to weave a web of romance around the tall yellow-bearded man with the sad eyes and the voice that gives itself perfectly to plaintive little Swedish songs remembered out of childhood. In the winter evenings we play chess together, he and I, and after some close, fierce battle has been fought to a finish—usually with my own defeat—we fill our pipes again, and Ehrensvärd tells me stories of the far, half-remembered days in the fatherland, before he went to sea: stories that grow very strange and incredible as the night deepens and the fire falls together, but stories that, nevertheless, I fully believe.

One of them made a strong impression on me, so I set it down here, only regretting that I cannot reproduce the curiously perfect English and the delicate accent which to me increased the fascination of the tale. Yet, as best I can remember it, here it is.

"I never told you how Nils and I went over the hills to Hallsberg, and how we found the Dead Valley, did I? Well, this is the way it happened. I must have been about twelve years old, and Nils Sjöberg, whose father's estate joined ours, was a few months younger. We were inseparable just at that time, and whatever we did, we did together.

"Once a week it was market day in Engelholm, and Nils and I went always there to see the strange sights that the market gathered from all the surrounding country. One day we quite lost our hearts, for an old man from across the Elfborg had brought a little dog to sell, that seemed to us the most beautiful dog in all the world. He was a round, woolly puppy, so funny that Nils and I sat down on the ground and laughed at him, until he came and played with us in so jolly a way that we felt that there was only one really desirable thing in life, and that was the little dog of the old man from across the hills. But alas! we had not half money enough wherewith to buy him, so we were forced to beg the old man not to sell him before the next market day, promising that we would bring the money for him then. He gave us his word, and we ran home very fast and implored our mothers to give us money for the little dog.

"We got the money, but we could not wait for the next market day. Suppose the puppy should be sold! The thought frightened us so that we begged and implored that we might be allowed to go over the hills to Hallsberg where the old man lived, and get the little dog ourselves, and at last they told us we might go. By starting early in the morning we should reach Hallsberg by three o'clock, and it was arranged that we should stay there that night with Nils's aunt, and, leaving by noon the next day, be home again by sunset.

"Soon after sunrise we were on our way, after having received minute instructions as to just what we should do in all possible and impossible circumstances, and finally a repeated injunction that we should start for home at the same hour the next day, so that we might get safely back before nightfall.

"For us, it was magnificent sport, and we started off with our rifles, full of the sense of our very great importance: yet the journey was simple enough, along a good road, across the big hills we knew so well, for Nils and I had shot over half the territory this side of the dividing ridge of the Elfborg. Back of Engelholm lay a long valley, from which rose the low mountains, and we had to cross this, and then follow the road along the side of the hills for three or four miles, before a narrow path branched off to the left, leading up through the pass.

"Nothing occurred of interest on the way over, and we reached Hallsberg in due season, found to our inexpressible joy that the little dog was not sold, secured him, and so went to the house of Nils's aunt to spend the night.

"Why we did not leave early on the following day, I can't quite remember; at all events, I know we stopped at a shooting range just outside of the town, where most attractive pasteboard pigs were sliding slowly through painted foliage, serving so as beautiful marks. The result was that we did not get fairly started for home until afternoon, and as we found ourselves at last pushing up the side of the mountain with the sun dangerously near their summits, I think we were a little scared at the prospect of the examination and possible punishment that awaited us when we got home at midnight.

"Therefore we hurried as fast as possible up the mountain side, while the blue dusk closed in about us, and the light died in the purple sky. At first we had talked hilariously, and the little dog had leaped ahead of us with the utmost joy. Latterly, however, a curious oppression came on us; we did not speak or even whistle, while the dog fell behind, following us with hesitation in every muscle.

"We had passed through the foothills and the low spurs of the mountains, and were almost at the top of the main range, when life seemed to go out of everything, leaving the world dead, so suddenly silent the forest became, so stagnant the air. Instinctively we halted to listen.

"Perfect silence,—the crushing silence of deep forests at night; and more, for always, even in the most impenetrable fastnesses of the wooded mountains, is the multitudinous murmur of little lives, awakened by the darkness, exaggerated and intensified by the stillness of the air and the great dark: but here and now the silence seemed unbroken even by the turn of a leaf, the movement of a twig, the note of night bird or insect. I could hear the blood beat through my veins; and the crushing of the grass under our feet as we advanced with hesitating steps sounded like the falling of trees.

"And the air was stagnant,—dead. The atmosphere seemed to lie upon the body like the weight of sea on a diver who has ventured too far into its awful depths. What we usually call silence seems so only in relation to the din of ordinary experience. This was silence in the absolute, and it crushed the mind while it intensified the senses, bringing down the awful weight of inextinguishable fear.

"I know that Nils and I stared towards each other in abject terror, listening to our quick, heavy breathing, that sounded to our acute senses like the fitful rush of waters. And the poor little dog we were leading justified our terror. The black oppression seemed to crush him even as it did us. He lay close on the ground, moaning feebly, and dragging himself painfully and slowly closer to Nils's feet. I think this exhibition of utter animal fear was the last touch, and must inevitably have blasted our reason—mine anyway; but just then, as we stood quaking on the bounds of madness, came a sound, so awful, so ghastly, so horrible, that it seemed to rouse us from the dead spell that was on us.

"In the depth of the silence came a cry, beginning as a low, sorrowful moan, rising to a tremulous shriek, culminating in a yell that seemed to tear the night in sunder and rend the world as by a cataclysm. So fearful was it that I could not believe it had actual existence: it passed previous experience, the powers of belief, and for a moment I thought it the result of my own animal terror, an hallucination born of tottering reason.

"A glance at Nils dispelled this thought in a flash. In the pale light of the high stars he was the embodiment of all possible human fear, quaking with an ague, his jaw fallen, his tongue out, his eyes protruding like those of a hanged man. Without a word we fled, the panic of fear giving us strength, and together, the little dog caught close in Nils's arms, we sped down the side of the cursed mountains,—anywhere, goal was of no account: we had but one impulse—to get away from that place.

"So under the black trees and the far white stars that flashed through the still leaves overhead, we leaped down the mountain side, regardless of path or landmark, straight through the tangled underbrush, across mountain streams, through fens and copses, anywhere, so only that our course was downward.

"How long we ran thus, I have no idea, but by and by the forest fell behind, and we found ourselves among the foothills, and fell exhausted on the dry short grass, panting like tired dogs.

"It was lighter here in the open, and presently we looked around to see where we were, and how we were to strike out in order to find the path that would lead us home. We looked in vain for a familiar sign. Behind us rose the great wall of black forest on the flank of the mountain: before us lay the undulating mounds of low foothills, unbroken by trees or rocks, and beyond, only the fall of black sky bright with multitudinous stars that turned its velvet depth to a luminous gray.

"As I remember, we did not speak to each other once: the terror was too heavy on us for that, but by and by we rose simultaneously and started out across the hills.

"Still the same silence, the same dead, motionless air—air that was at once sultry and chilling: a heavy heat struck through with an icy chill that felt almost like the burning of frozen steel. Still carrying the helpless dog, Nils pressed on through the hills, and I followed close behind. At last, in front of us, rose a slope of moor touching the white stars. We climbed it wearily, reached the top, and found ourselves gazing down into a great, smooth valley, filled half way to the brim with—what?

"As far as the eye could see stretched a level plain of ashy white, faintly phosphorescent, a sea of velvet fog that lay like motionless water, or rather like a floor of alabaster, so dense did it appear, so seemingly capable of sustaining weight. If it were possible, I think that sea of dead white mist struck even greater terror into my soul than the heavy silence or the deadly cry—so ominous was it, so utterly unreal, so phantasmal, so impossible, as it lay there like a dead ocean under the steady stars. Yet through that mist *we must go*! there seemed no other way home, and, shattered with abject fear, mad with the one desire to get back, we started down the slope to where the sea of milky mist ceased, sharp and distinct around the stems of the rough grass.

"I put one foot into the ghostly fog. A chill as of death struck through me, stopping my heart, and I threw myself backward on the slope. At that instant came again the shriek, close, close, right in our ears, in ourselves, and far out across that damnable sea I saw the cold fog lift like a water-spout and toss itself high in writhing convolutions towards the sky. The stars began to grow dim as thick vapour swept across them, and in the growing dark I saw a great, watery moon lift itself slowly above the palpitating sea, vast and vague in the gathering mist.

"This was enough: we turned and fled along the margin of the white sea that throbbed now with fitful motion below us, rising, rising, slowly and steadily, driving us higher and higher up the side of the foothills.

"It was a race for life; that we knew. How we kept it up I cannot understand, but we did, and at last we saw the white sea fall behind us as we staggered up the end of the valley, and then down into a region that we knew, and so into the old path. The last thing I remember was hearing a strange voice, that of Nils, but horribly changed, stammer brokenly, 'The dog is dead!' and then the whole world turned around twice, slowly and resistlessly, and consciousness went out with a crash.

"It was some three weeks later, as I remember, that I awoke in my own room, and found my mother sitting beside the bed. I could not think very well at first, but as I slowly grew strong again, vague flashes of recollection began to come to me, and little by little the whole sequence of events of that awful night in the Dead Valley came back. All that I could gain from what was told me was that three weeks before I had been found in my own bed, raging sick, and that my illness grew fast into brain fever. I tried to speak of the dread things that had happened to me, but I saw at once that no one looked on them save as the hauntings of a dying frenzy, and so I closed my mouth and kept my own counsel.

"I must see Nils, however, and so I asked for him. My mother told me that he also had been ill with a strange fever, but that he was now quite well again. Presently they brought him in, and when we were alone I began to speak to him of the night on the mountain. I shall never forget the shock that struck me down on my pillow when the boy denied everything: denied having gone with me, ever having heard the cry, having seen the valley, or feeling the deadly chill of the ghostly fog. Nothing would shake his determined ignorance, and in spite of myself I was forced to admit that his denials came from no policy of concealment, but from blank oblivion.

"My weakened brain was in a turmoil. Was it all but the floating phantasm of delirium? Or had the horror of the real thing blotted Nils's mind into blankness so far as the events of the night in the Dead Valley were concerned? The latter explanation seemed the only one, else how explain the sudden illness which in a night had struck us both down? I said nothing more, either to Nils or to my own people, but waited, with a growing determination that, once well again, I would find that valley if it really existed.

"It was some weeks before I was really well enough to go, but finally, late in September, I chose a bright, warm, still day, the last smile of the dying summer, and started early in the morning along the path that led to Hallsberg. I was sure I knew where the trail struck off to the right, down which we had come from the valley of dead water, for a great tree grew by the Hallsberg path at the point where, with a sense of salvation, we had found the home road. Presently I saw it to the right, a little distance ahead.

"I think the bright sunlight and the clear air had worked as a tonic to me, for by the time I came to the foot of the great pine, I had quite lost faith in the verity of the vision that haunted me, believing at last that it was indeed but the nightmare of madness. Nevertheless, I turned sharply to the right, at the base of the tree, into a narrow path that led through a dense thicket. As I did so I tripped over something. A swarm of flies sung into the air around me, and looking down I saw the matted fleece, with the poor little bones thrusting through, of the dog we had bought in Hallsberg.

"Then my courage went out with a puff, and I knew that it all was true, and that now I was frightened. Pride and the desire for adventure urged me on, however, and I pressed into the close thicket that barred my way. The path was hardly visible: merely the worn road of some small beasts, for, though it showed in the crisp grass, the bushes above grew thick and hardly penetrable. The land rose slowly, and rising grew clearer, until at last I came out on a great slope of hill, unbroken by trees or shrubs, very like my memory of that rise of land we had topped in order that we might find the dead valley and the icy fog. I looked at the sun; it was bright and clear, and all around insects were humming in the autumn air, and birds were darting to and fro. Surely there was no danger, not until nightfall at least; so I began to whistle, and with a rush mounted the last crest of brown hill.

"There lay the Dead Valley! A great oval basin, almost as smooth and regular as though made by man. On all sides the grass crept over the brink of the encircling hills, dusty green on the crests, then fading into ashy brown, and so to a deadly white, this last colour forming a thin ring, running in a long line around the slope. And then? Nothing. Bare, brown, hard earth, glittering with grains of alkali, but otherwise dead and barren. Not a tuft of grass, not a stick of brushwood, not even a stone, but only the vast expanse of beaten clay.

"In the midst of the basin, perhaps a mile and a half away, the level expanse was broken by a great dead tree, rising leafless and gaunt into the air. Without a moment's hesitation I started down into the valley and made for this goal. Every particle of fear seemed to have left me, and even the valley itself did not look so very terrifying. At all events, I was driven by an over-whelming curiosity, and there seemed to be but one thing in the world to do,—to get to that Tree! As I trudged along over the hard earth, I noticed that the multitudinous voices of birds and insects had died away. No bee or butterfly hovered through the air, no insects leaped or crept over the dull earth. The very air itself was stagnant.

"As I drew near the skeleton tree, I noticed the glint of sunlight on a kind of white mound around its roots, and I wondered curiously. It was not until I had come close that I saw its nature.

"All around the roots and barkless trunk was heaped a wilderness of little bones. Tiny skulls of rodents and of birds, thousands of them, rising about the dead tree and streaming off for several yards in all directions, until the dreadful pile ended in isolated skulls and scattered skeletons. Here and there a larger bone appeared,—the thigh of a sheep, the hoofs of a horse, and to one side, grinning slowly, a human skull.

"I stood quite still, staring with all my eyes, when suddenly the dense silence was broken by a faint, forlorn cry high over my head. I looked up and saw a great falcon turning and sailing downward just over the tree. In a moment more she fell motionless on the bleaching bones.

"Horror struck me, and I rushed for home, my brain whirling, a strange numbness growing in me. I ran steadily, on and on. At last I glanced up. Where was the rise of hill? I looked around wildly. Close before me was the dead tree with its pile of bones. I had circled it round and round, and the valley wall was still a mile and a half away.

"I stood dazed and frozen. The sun was sinking, red and dull, towards the line of hills. In the east the dark was growing fast. Was there still time? *Time!* It was not *that* I wanted, it was *will!* My feet seemed clogged as in a nightmare. I could hardly drag them over the barren earth. And then I felt the slow chill creeping through me. I looked down. Out of the earth a thin mist was rising, collecting in little pools that grew ever larger until they joined here and there, their currents swirling slowly like thin blue smoke. The western hills halved the copper sun. When it was dark I should hear that shriek again, and then I should die. I knew that, and with every remaining atom of will I staggered towards the red west through the writhing mist that crept clammily around my ankles, retarding my steps.

"And as I fought my way off from the Tree, the horror grew, until at last I thought I was going to die. The silence pursued me like dumb ghosts, the still air held my breath, the hellish fog caught at my feet like cold hands.

"But I won! though not a moment too soon. As I crawled on my hands and knees up the brown slope, I heard, far away and high in the air, the cry that already had almost bereft me of reason. It was faint and vague, but unmistakable in its horrible intensity. I glanced behind. The fog was dense and pallid, heaving undulously up the brown slope. The sky was gold under the setting sun, but below was the ashy gray of death. I stood for a moment on the brink of this sea of hell, and then leaped down the slope. The sunset opened before me, the night closed behind, and as I crawled home weak and tired, darkness shut down on the Dead Valley."

Postscript

There seem to be certain well-defined roots existing in all countries, from which spring the current legends of the supernatural; and therefore for the germs of the stories in this book the Author claims no originality. These legends differ one from the other only in local colour and in individual treatment. If the Author has succeeded in clothing one or two of these norms in some slightly new vesture, he is more than content.

Boston, July 3, 1895.

LEONAUR

ALSO FROM LEONAUR
AVAILABLE IN SOFTCOVER OR HARDCOVER WITH DUST JACKET

THE COLLECTED SUPERNATURAL AND WEIRD FICTION OF J. SHERIDAN LE FANU: VOLUME 1 *by J. Sheridan le Fanu*—Contains Two Novels 'The Haunted Baronet' and 'The Evil Guest', One Novella 'Carmilla',One Novelette and Ten Short Stories of the Ghostly and Gothic.

THE COLLECTED SUPERNATURAL AND WEIRD FICTION OF J. SHERIDAN LE FANU: VOLUME 2 *by J. Sheridan le Fanu*—Contains One Novel 'Uncle Silas', One Novelette 'Green Tea' and Five Short Stories of the Ghostly and Gothic.

THE COLLECTED SUPERNATURAL AND WEIRD FICTION OF J. SHERIDAN LE FANU: VOLUME 3 *by J. Sheridan le Fanu*—Contains One Novel 'The House by the Churchyard', and One Short Story 'Dickon the Devil' of the Ghostly and Gothic.

THE COLLECTED SUPERNATURAL AND WEIRD FICTION OF J. SHERIDAN LE FANU: VOLUME 4 *by J. Sheridan le Fanu*—Contains One Novel 'The Wyvern Mystery', One Novelette 'Mr. Justice Harbottle,' and Nine Short Stories of the Ghostly and Gothic.

THE COLLECTED SUPERNATURAL AND WEIRD FICTION OF J. SHERIDAN LE FANU: VOLUME 5 *by J. Sheridan le Fanu*—Contains One Novel 'The Rose and the Key', One Novelette 'Spalatro, From the Notes of Fra Giacomo', and Two Short Stories of the Ghostly and Gothic

THE COLLECTED SUPERNATURAL AND WEIRD FICTION OF J. SHERIDAN LE FANU: VOLUME 6 *by J. Sheridan le Fanu*—Contains One Novel 'Checkmate', and Six Short Stories of the Ghostly and Gothic

THE COLLECTED SUPERNATURAL AND WEIRD FICTION OF J. SHERIDAN LE FANU: VOLUME 7 *by J. Sheridan le Fanu*—Contains Two Novels 'All in the Dark' and 'The Room in the Dragon Volant', Two Novelettes 'The Mysterious Lodger' and 'The Watcher' and Four Short Stories of the Ghostly and Gothic

THE COLLECTED SUPERNATURAL AND WEIRD FICTION OF J. SHERIDAN LE FANU: VOLUME 8 *by J. Sheridan le Fanu*—Contains One Novel 'A Lost Name', One Novelette 'The Last Heir of Castle Connor', and Six Short Stoies of the Ghostly and Gothic

LEONAUR

ALSO FROM LEONAUR
AVAILABLE IN SOFTCOVER OR HARDCOVER WITH DUST JACKET

THE COMPLETE FOUR JUST MEN: VOLUME 2 *by Edgar Wallace*—*The Law of the Four Just Men & The Three Just Men*—disillusioned with a world where the wicked and the abusers of power perpetually go unpunished, the Just Men set about to rectify matters according to their own standards, and retribution is dispensed on swift and deadly wings.

THE COMPLETE RAFFLES: 1 *by E. W. Hornung*—*The Amateur Cracksman & The Black Mask*—By turns urbane gentleman about town and accomplished cricketer, life is just too ordinary for Raffles and that sets him on a series of adventures that have long been treasured as a real antidote to the 'white knights' who are the usual heroes of the crime fiction of this period.

THE COMPLETE RAFFLES: 2 *by E. W. Hornung*—*A Thief in the Night & Mr Justice Raffles*—By turns urbane gentleman about town and accomplished cricketer, life is just too ordinary for Raffles and that sets him on a series of adventures that have long been treasured as a real antidote to the 'white knights' who are the usual heroes of the crime fiction of this period.

THE COLLECTED SUPERNATURAL AND WEIRD FICTION OF WILKIE COLLINS: VOLUME 1 *by Wilkie Collins*—Contains one novel 'The Haunted Hotel', one novella 'Mad Monkton', three novelettes 'Mr Percy and the Prophet', 'The Biter Bit' and 'The Dead Alive' and eight short stories to chill the blood.

THE COLLECTED SUPERNATURAL AND WEIRD FICTION OF WILKIE COLLINS: VOLUME 2 *by Wilkie Collins*—Contains one novel 'The Two Destinies', three novellas 'The Frozen deep', 'Sister Rose' and 'The Yellow Mask' and two short stories to chill the blood.

THE COLLECTED SUPERNATURAL AND WEIRD FICTION OF WILKIE COLLINS: VOLUME 3 *by Wilkie Collins*—Contains one novel 'Dead Secret,' two novelettes 'Mrs Zant and the Ghost' and 'The Nun's Story of Gabriel's Marriage' and five short stories to chill the blood.

FUNNY BONES *selected by Dorothy Scarborough*—An Anthology of Humorous Ghost Stories.

MONTEZUMA'S CASTLE AND OTHER WEIRD TALES *by Charles B. Cory*—Cory has written a superb collection of eighteen ghostly and weird stories to chill and thrill the avid enthusiast of supernatural fiction.

SUPERNATURAL BUCHAN *by John Buchan*—Stories of Ancient Spirits, Uncanny Places & Strange Creatures.

LEONAUR

ALSO FROM LEONAUR

AVAILABLE IN SOFTCOVER OR HARDCOVER WITH DUST JACKET

MR MUKERJI'S GHOSTS *by S. Mukerji*—Supernatural tales from the British Raj period by India's Ghost story collector.

KIPLINGS GHOSTS *by Rudyard Kipling*—Twelve stories of Ghosts, Hauntings, Curses, Werewolves & Magic.

THE COLLECTED SUPERNATURAL AND WEIRD FICTION OF WASHINGTON IRVING: VOLUME 1 *by Washington Irving*—Including one novel 'A History of New York', and nine short stories of the Strange and Unusual.

THE COLLECTED SUPERNATURAL AND WEIRD FICTION OF WASHINGTON IRVING: VOLUME 2 *by Washington Irving*—Including three novelettes 'The Legend of the Sleepy Hollow', 'Dolph Heyliger', 'The Adventure of the Black Fisherman' and thirty-two short stories of the Strange and Unusual.

THE COLLECTED SUPERNATURAL AND WEIRD FICTION OF JOHN KENDRICK BANGS: VOLUME 1 *by John Kendrick Bangs*—Including one novel 'Toppleton's Client or A Spirit in Exile', and ten short stories of the Strange and Unusual.

THE COLLECTED SUPERNATURAL AND WEIRD FICTION OF JOHN KENDRICK BANGS: VOLUME 2 *by John Kendrick Bangs*—Including four novellas 'A House-Boat on the Styx', 'The Pursuit of the House-Boat', 'The Enchanted Typewriter' and 'Mr. Munchausen' of the Strange and Unusual.

THE COLLECTED SUPERNATURAL AND WEIRD FICTION OF JOHN KENDRICK BANGS: VOLUME 3 *by John Kendrick Bangs*—Including twor novellas 'Olympian Nights', 'Roger Camerden: A Strange Story', and ten short stories of the Strange and Unusual.

THE COLLECTED SUPERNATURAL AND WEIRD FICTION OF MARY SHELLEY: VOLUME 1 *by Mary Shelley*—Including one novel 'Frankenstein or the Modern Prometheus', and fourteen short stories of the Strange and Unusual.

THE COLLECTED SUPERNATURAL AND WEIRD FICTION OF MARY SHELLEY: VOLUME 2 *by Mary Shelley*—Including one novel 'The Last Man', and three short stories of the Strange and Unusual.

THE COLLECTED SUPERNATURAL AND WEIRD FICTION OF AMELIA B. EDWARDS *by Amelia B. Edwards*—Contains two novelettes 'Monsieur Maurice', and 'The Discovery of the Treasure Isles', one ballad 'A Legend of Boisguilbert' and seventeen short stories to cill the blood.